Temple Israel Library
Minneapolis, Minn.

Please sign your full name on the above card.

Return books promptly to the Library or Temple Office.

Fines will be charged for overdue books or for damage or loss of same.

DEMCO

The Whispering Mezuzah
and other
Devora Doresh Mysteries

by

Carol Korb Hubner

Illustrated by

Devorah Kramer

Judaica Press • 1979
New York

MANUFACTURED IN THE UNITED STATES OF AMERICA

Contents

This book is dedicated to
My Husband
lifetime companion,
who encourages me with
patience, devotion and good humor

The Whispering Mezuzah

itting in the back seat of the family car, Devora Doresh stared blankly out of the window at the passing scenery consisting of trees and shrubs adorned with their autumnal finery. For a city girl like Devora, the ride into the country promised to be very exciting, but after two hours of watching trees and shrubs fly by, Devora became bored.

Sitting near the opposite window, her little brother, Chaim, flattened his nose against the glass as he leaned on the door in a trance-like state, staring at the same scenery. Occasionally, he would blow softly at the window causing the glass to steam, and then he would inhale and watch the vapor disappear.

Devora's father, Rebbe Doresh, sat low in the passenger side of the front seat, sleeping soundly, his yarmulke tilted over his right ear. His left arm was in a cast and rested on his stomach. Devora's mother was at the wheel, her head dropping slowly to her chest as she grew drowsy from the trip. She was being hypnotized by the dotted white lines which rushed at the car along the middle of the road, and soon the car began swerving slightly.

Mrs. Doresh shook her head to keep herself awake. She was, however, unsuccessful, and the car continued to swerve.

Rebbe Doresh suddenly awoke, and realized the danger they were in. He realized too that he would have to talk to his wife in order to keep her awake. "You know, I've been thinking," he said, yawning. "I feel better about this trip now. I was a little disappointed that we weren't spending *Sukkos*[1] at home. But what can I do? With my arm out of commission, I can't possibly build a *sukkah*. Your sister Baila's invitation was a G-dsend, and could not have come at a better time. But I was thinking of how we could use this stay in the country anyway. It will do us a world of good. The fresh air, I mean. The wide open spaces. The beautiful scenery."

"Look over there," said Mrs. Doresh, pointing towards the windshield. "Someone's waving a handkerchief. Maybe he needs help. He's got a van parked on the side of the road and it seems to be smoking."

Chaim leaned forward to see.

"Why should we help?" He asked. Rebbe Doresh turned around. "Will you please sit back, Chaim? Of course, a Jew is supposed to assist anyone in need."

"Anyone? Even a criminal?" Chaim asked.

"Well, in the case of a criminal, you're supposed to help all the innocent people around by having him

1. Tabernacles—a Jewish Festival.

locked up. Everything has to be examined within its own context, Chaim."

The car pulled off the road onto the grass. Rebbe Doresh rolled down his window as the driver of the van approached.

"Thanks for stopping, mister," the man said, wiping his forehead with the handkerchief. "Sure glad you folks came along. The engine overheated. Guess they didn't put in enough water at the garage. You folks got some water by any chance? I'm pretty sure that's all the old machine needs to stop smoking and get back on the road."

Rebbe Doresh stepped out of the car and walked towards the trunk. The man wiped his brow again and glanced at the cast on Rebbe Doresh's arm. "Pheeeeeeeew," he sighed. "Where did you get that?"

Rebbe Doresh opened the trunk.

"This car?" He asked.

"No. That arm."

"Oh, the cast. I fell down the steps on my way down to the cellar. Thank G-d that is all that happened to me."

Rebbe Doresh removed a gallon of water from the trunk and handed it to the man.

"Thank G-d?" the man asked, puzzled. "Why would you want to thank G-d for an accident?"

"Because it could have been much worse."

"You really believe that G-d helped you?"

"Yes."

"Well, don't you think he could have helped you in a better way, by preventing the fall altogether?"

"Certainly," Rebbe Doresh said with a smile, as he accompanied the man to the van. "But this is not paradise, you know. There's a great deal in life that we control ourselves. That goes for safety as well. A person cannot say, 'I'll just walk with my eyes shut, and G-d will watch out for me,' but he must use the senses G-d gave him in order to prevent himself from stumbling. I'm sure I could have been more careful than I was when I fell down those stairs. But even though I may have caused the accident, G-d protected me from hurting myself too much. I could have broken my legs, or my head, too, but I didn't."

The man began pouring the water into his radiator.

"That's very interesting," he said, escorting Rebbe Doresh back to the trunk. Rebbe Doresh returned the empty container to the trunk and slammed it shut over the luggage.

"It'll probably take a few minutes to cool off," the man remarked.

"That's okay," Rebbe Doresh said, leaning back against the car. "We'll wait with you a few moments to make sure. If it doesn't work out, we can always drive to the nearest service station and let them know you're here."

"Thanks a million," the man said, wiping his brow. "I really appreciate all this. You people from around these parts?"

"No, are you?"

"Nope. I'm just out here making a delivery. And you wouldn't believe what I'm delivering."

Rebbe Doresh smiled.

"What are you delivering?"

"Listen to this: sand."

"Sand?" Devora asked from inside the car. The man bent over and looked past Rebbe Doresh, into the back seat of the car.

"That's right, young lady. Sand."

"What are you? A builder?" She asked. Rebbe Doresh chuckled.

"Nope. I'm just delivering the stuff." He stood erect and turned back to Rebbe Doresh. "Would you believe it? I'm delivering sand, for some kind of convention."

"Convention?" Cried Devora. "Sand at a convention?"

The man reached into his shirt pocket and removed some invoices.

"Yeah. Says right here. Uh . . . Antique Gold Collector's Convention." He put the papers back into his pocket. "Right here in the mountains. Would you believe such a thing? Sand! The guy calls up and says 'Hello? Mercer here. Send me sand,' he says; and this guy Mercer's supposed to be a real biggie. 'Big Frank' they call him. 'French sand,' he says, hear that? 'the finest sand you got,' he says. So, what do I do? No questions asked. I just deliver."

"Well," Rebbe Doresh said, "sand is somehow used

in the gold-melting process, I think, isn't it?"

"Beats me, mister. I just deliver. I don't care what they do with that sand."

The man walked back to the van and peered into the radiator.

"Looks like it's simmered down. I'm going to try it out." He climbed into the driver's seat and turned on the ignition. The engine responded normally.

"Sounds okay." He yelled.

Rebbe Doresh returned to his seat in the car and pulled the door shut.

As Mrs. Doresh pulled off the grass and back onto the road, the man shouted at them from his van.

"Hey, you guys! Thanks a lot again!"

Rebbe Doresh shouted back: "Thank G-d, too! It could have been worse!"

The man stared at the Doresh car in puzzlement as it disappeared down the road.

"It's a good thing we brought some water along," Rebbe Doresh remarked.

"At first I wasn't going to," Mrs. Doresh said. "I mean, I didn't think we would ever need it since we have a special cooling liquid in our tank to prevent overheating. But then I remembered what my father used to teach us: always take along some extra food and money; if *you* don't need it, maybe someone else will. I'll never forget that. He'd even carry extra tissue paper with him when he would just ride on the city bus. And then you should have seen it. Someone would sneeze and sit there helplessly when my father would run over with the tissues."

Everyone laughed.

"Nothing could have happened to this car anyhow," Devora said. "Isn't it true, Abba, that when you're on your way to do a *mitzvah*,[2] no harm could befall you?"

"True," Rebbe Doresh said. "This is what we are taught in the Talmud."

"Well, first of all, we're on our way to observe the the commandment of living in a *sukkah,* right? And second of all, we're also delivering new *mezuzos* for Uncle Shlomo's house, right? So the car would have been safe either way even if we didn't have the coolant in the radiator."

"Yes," Rebbe Doresh said. "But at the same time, the Torah also teaches us we should not depend upon miracles. A person must do whatever he can, make every possible human effort on his part first, and not sit idly back and rely on G-d. G-d wants us to make the first move. When we do everything we possibly can and still need help, then we can ask for miracles. A very important rule."

"Hey, yeah!" Chaim shouted excitedly. "That's like what we learned last week in *yeshiva*. The *Midrash*[3] says that the Red Sea didn't split for the Jewish people till

2. Good deed.
3. Talmudic explanations of the Bible.

the tribes went into the water and kept walking till the water reached their nostrils."

"Right," Rebbe Doresh beamed. "Good example, Chaim."

"Abba," Devora said. "Why are we bringing Uncle Shlomo new *mezuzos?* Doesn't he have any?"

"He has," Mrs. Doresh answered. "When they moved in to the house, the owner already had *mezuzos* on the doors. But *mezuzos* have to be examined at least twice every seven years, and when Uncle Shlomo checked them last week, he found that the letters on some of the parchments were cracked in several places."

"So why didn't he buy new ones right away?" Devora asked.

"He wasn't feeling well this week and couldn't make the trip all the way into the city to get some new ones, so . . ."

"Wait!" shouted Chaim, "But aren't you not allowed to live in a house without a kosher *mezuzah?*"

"True," Mrs. Doresh said. "But the *halachah*[4] is that as long as you intend to get some proper ones at the first opportunity, you are not violating the commandment. This is a general rule, if a person intended to do a *mitzvah* but was prevented from doing it by circumstances beyond his control, it is considered as if he actually did it. Uncle Shlomo was unable to make a trip to buy the *mezuzos,* but he took advantage of the first opportunity;

4. Jewish law.

when he heard we were planning to come up for *Sukkos,* he asked us to buy the new *mezuzos* for him."

"Can I see them?" Chaim cried. "Can I? Can I?" Rebbe Doresh opened the glove compartment and withdrew a small white box. He held it behind his head so that Chaim could take it. Devora inched her way over to where Chaim was seated and the two peered into the box.

"Where are they?" Chaim cried, a little disappointed. "These are little tiny *megillahs!*[5] Where are the *mezuzos?*"

"Those are *mezuzos,*" Devora said, smiling. "These are rolled up parchments on which the commandment of *mezuzah* is written."

"But I thought *mezuzos* were made of gold or silver or wood or plastic!" Chaim protested.

"That's the *case,* Chaim," Devora explained. "That's just the outer case which contains the real *mezuzah.*"

"What does it say?"

"It's the first two paragraphs of the *Sh'ma,*[6] both of which teach us the commandment of having a *mezuzah* on our doorposts."

"We also have these words in our *tefillin,*[7]" Rebbe Doresh added. "Because these two paragraphs also tell about the commandment to wear *tefillin.*"

5. Scrolls.
6. A prayer (see Glossary).
7. Phylacteries.

"And so a *mezuzah* is supposed to protect us?"
Asked Chaim.

"Well," Rebbe Doresh explained. "The *Rambam*[8]
teaches us not to look at the *mezuzah* as a protection,
but rather as a reminder of our responsibilities to G-d. If
we do our part, G-d will do His, and take care of us."

"How come there are only four *mezuzos* in the
box?" asked Devora. "Don't they have twelve rooms?"

"Yes," Mrs. Doresh replied. "But when Aunt Baila
called, she said the rest of the *mezuzos* were kosher and
met the requirements. They only needed four."

Chaim sat up in his seat and leaned forward, tapping
his father's left shoulder. Rebbe Doresh turned around
and smiled.

"Yes, Chaim, what is it?"

"Abba, remember you once told me a story from
the Talmud about Onkelos and the *mezuzah?* Remember? Tell it to me again. Please, Abba."

"Okay, Chaim," Rebbe Doresh said. "I'll tell it to
you. But first you must sit back. It's not safe what
you're doing. Your mother could make a sudden stop
and you could bump your head against the back of the
seat, unless you're sitting back."

Chaim complied and sat back, eager to hear the
story. Rebbe Doresh took Chaim back more than 1,900
years ago to the time of Onkelos, a nephew of the
emperor of Rome. Onkelos was very impressed by the

8. Maimonides—famous Jewish sage and physician.

Jewish people when he visited them after Rome had invaded Israel and destroyed the Second Temple. He wished to learn Torah and decided to become Jewish. Eventually he became a great Torah sage, and his translation of the Torah into Aramaic is studied to this day. When Onkelos first decided to become a Jew, his family in Rome was very disturbed and they immediately sent troops to bring him back home. But with each shipment of troops, Onkelos succeeded in talking them out of their mission and into becoming Jews, too. Finally, the family sent one last group of soldiers to seize Onkelos, but this time they ordered the soldiers not to talk to him, just to bring him back to Rome.

The soldiers complied. They took Onkelos and escorted him out of his home in Eretz Israel. As he walked out of the door with the soldiers, he stopped and kissed the *mezuzah* on the doorpost. The soldiers could not resist asking him why he was kissing that strange object on the doorpost, so they questioned him. Onkelos then began telling them about the greatness of Hashem. He told them how different the King of the Universe is from the King of Rome. "The ruler of Rome sits inside his palace while his servants guard the door. The ruler of the universe, Hashem, guards the doors of His servants while they sit inside." The soldiers were so impressed by his words that they, too, decided to become Jews.

Rebbe Doresh finished the story and turned around to watch Chaim's reaction to the story. A big smile formed across Chaim's face. He then turned to Devora.

"Now *you* tell me a *mezuzah* story. You know, the one you told me when I was sick, you know, about Abba Arika, also known as Rav, the great rabbi in Babylonia, remember?"

Devora cleared her throat and began telling Chaim about the sultan, Artaban and how he once tested the loyalty and wisdom of the Jewish leader of his country, Rav. Artaban sent the rabbi a huge treasure chest filled with gold, silver, and rubies. He then sat back and waited to see how the rabbi could possibly repay him for the gift.

Soon a messenger arrived at the palace and announced that he had been sent by Rav with a special gift for his royal highness. Artaban was very eager to see what he would get and ran to the messenger. The messenger gave him a very small box. The sultan opened it and grew angry. "What's this?" He shouted. He ordered the messenger to go back and bring the rabbi for an explanation. Soon, Rav was brought before the sultan and the sultan demanded to know what the object in the box was all about.

"This is a *mezuzah*" the rabbi explained. The sultan was furious. "I give you gold, silver and rubies, and you give me a little metal box?" The sultan was very upset, but the rabbi remained calm.

"Your highness," he said. "Yes, you gave me a gift of diamonds and rubies, a gift which I may have today and may not have tomorrow. I gave you a *mezuzah,* which is a blessing from *Hashem* that he will always watch over you and protect you. Today and tomorrow. Now, is not my gift the greater one?"

The sultan was extremely impressed by Rav's words and appointed him as his Chief Advisor.

Again Chaim smiled with pride. He loved nothing better than to listen to stories of Jewish heroes who accomplished more with their knowledge of Torah than other heroes accomplished with their muscles.

Mrs. Doresh was smiling. Devora noticed her mother's grin in the rear-view mirror. She was up to something, Devora thought to herself. Her mother knew something the others did not.

"What's so funny, mommy?" Devora finally asked.

"Well, nothing really," she answered. "I was just thinking, now it's my turn to tell a *mezuzah* story."

Everyone turned to Mrs. Doresh eager to hear her story.

"Except that this story," she continued, "takes place today. And here to tell you the story, is the *mezuzah* itself."

The passengers all looked at one another, puzzled, and then watched Mrs. Doresh reach for a small *mezuzah* charm attached to the key chain which hung from the ignition. She grabbed the *mezuzah* and pressed on it. As she let go, everyone heard a strange sound coming from it: "Mashhhhhhh. Mashhhhhhh."

Everyone sat quietly, waiting for Mrs. Doresh to explain what was happening.

"I got it in the mail," she began. "Every year around *Rosh Hashanah*[9] and *Yom Kippur*[10] we always get different things in the mail from *yeshivos* or Jewish organizations trying to raise money. This year, this strange *mezuzah* key ring came in the mail from one of the yeshivos. I press it like this and it goes 'Mashhhhhhh.' What that means, I'll never guess. But it's cute."

"Devora will find out why," Chaim blurted. "She's the detective. Right, Devora?"

Devora smirked.

"This one is a real winner. What in the world could 'Mashhhhhhh' mean? Maybe it's just broken or something."

"I don't know," Mrs. Doresh said, smiling. "But at least you'll now have a mystery to solve while we're away from the excitement of city life. And once you've solved it, you'll have a fresh new *mezuzah* story to tell in addition to the ones about Onkelos and Rav."

The car slowed down as it entered a small town. The change of scenery was welcome to everyone and the family looked out their windows at the people walking on the narrow sidewalks and at the different stores.

"I don't see a kosher pizza shop," Chaim cried in dismay. Devora smiled at her brother and tapped him on the shoulder.

9. Jewish New Year.
10. Day of Atonement.

"You're only looking on one side of the street through your window. Don't jump to conclusions till you've looked out both windows."

Chaim moved over to Devora's side of the seat and peered out the window.

"Look! A kosher bakery!" He cried.

"And also pizza," Devora added. "Bracha wrote to me that they sell pizza there, too."

After a few minutes of driving through the main street, the car entered a residential section. Devora noticed how far apart the houses were, a welcome sight for a Brooklyn girl. There were tall trees standing close together all along the sidewalks and every home was surrounded by large areas of grass and smaller trees.

In the distance, Devora saw a very wide lake, its water sparkling in the sunlight and speckled with several small boats. A narrow strip of lawn edged away from the water with swathes of natural growth on either side of it and a large old house stood isolated near the lake, in the middle of a vast open space.

The car stopped a block before the lake. Devora looked at the home her father was pointing at and did a double-take. She looked back at the house near the lake. How strange, she thought. Uncle Shlomo's house looked exactly like the house near the lake!

Mrs. Doresh parked the car in front of the house. As they got out of the car and stretched their arms and legs, the Rabinowitz family ran out to greet them. Yankele skipped across the lawn towards Chaim, and the two of them ran off to the back yard. Devora spotted her cousin Bracha coming up the street with a bag of groceries that looked as though it weighed more than she did. Excusing herself, Devora ran to help her with the load.

"How was the trip?" Aunt Baila asked, as she gave her sister a hug. Mr. Rabinowitz was shaking Rebbe Doresh's hand very excitedly. "It's good to see you again," he said.

Aunt Baila bit her lower lip as Mrs. Doresh told her about the trip and about her husband's arm. Mrs. Doresh noticed that her sister looked pale and worried.

"Is there something wrong?" she asked Aunt Baila. Devora came over with Bracha, holding a half-gallon jar of grape juice in her arm.

"Did you hear what happened?" Devora asked her mother. Mrs. Doresh realized that Bracha must have informed Devora of whatever it was that had occurred.

"I may as well tell you," Aunt Baila said. "We had a break-in in the middle of the night."

"What?!" Mrs. Doresh was shocked and took her sister's hand to comfort her. "Someone broke into the house?"

"Yes. But thank G-d he didn't take anything. He broke into the *sukkah,* of all places. We have a permanent *sukkah* with a real door and lock and everything. It came with the house. The owner, Mr. Hirsch had it built, and all you have to do on *Sukkos* is roll up the roof and put on *schach.* Hear that? A removable roof."

"So someone broke into the *sukkah?*" Devora asked.

Mrs. Doresh smiled. "Here comes the detective," she said.

"Yes," Aunt Baila answered. "They could have broken into the house, too, but they didn't. And nothing is missing."

Uncle Shlomo and Rebbe Doresh joined the others.

"Seems like they tried to take the door off," Uncle Shlomo said. "He was trying for the hinges. Very strange."

"Did you call the police?" Devora asked.

"Yes," said Aunt Baila. "We had them here first thing this morning. They looked around and said they would investigate, and then took off."

"What could they do?" Uncle Shlomo said, frowning. "Nothing was taken and there were no fingerprints or any other evidence."

"Well, let's forget about it for now," interrupted Aunt Baila. "It's soon *Sukkos,* a happy time of the year, and we have to get everything ready."

Uncle Shlomo helped the family with their luggage while Aunt Baila then gave everyone a grand tour of the house. Entering the kitchen, the Doresh family were glad to find some snacks on the table waiting for them. A bowl of fruit stood on the table alongside some orange juice and a plate of cookies. Aunt Baila opened the refrigerator and took out some milk and a bottle of cold water.

"Very nice, Shlomo," Rebbe Doresh remarked, his eyes scanning the length and width of the adjoining living room.

"Ah!" sighed Mr. Rabinowitz. "Don't ask what we had to do to this place when we first moved in. Mr. Hirsch, the former owner, was an elderly man. He had no family, no children, just this house. And, you know, he had no energy or money to fix it up."

"Oh, so he probably was happy to sell the place."

"Surprisingly enough, he was pretty tough about it. He wouldn't sell it to us at first. He wanted to know more about us. He interrogated me week after week. He wanted us to rent it first, rather than buy it, as if he didn't want to part with the house."

"So why did he sell it to you later?" Devora asked, biting into an apple.

"He probably realized he didn't have much longer to live. He was a sick man. A very sick man . Always going to the hospital. Sure enough, he knew what was happening to him. Not more than three weeks after he sold us the house, he died. But I guess he wanted to make sure that we were the kind of people he wanted to own his house, before he would sell it to us."

Aunt Baila broke in. "He even stipulated to us that the house is ours only if we promised him never to sell it to anyone else but a Torah observant Jew."

"Not only that," Bracha said, shaking Devora's

arm, "but he gave my father this secret message on a piece of paper before he died!"

Rebbe Doresh laughed. "A secret message? Oh, come on."

"It's true," Aunt Baila said, rising from her seat. She disappeared into the living room and within moments she was back, holding a folded piece of paper in her hand.

"Shlomo went to visit Mr. Hirsch in the hospital," she explained. "After visiting hours, Mr. Hirsch gave him this note."

"Very mysterious," Uncle Shlomo said. "He couldn't speak any more when I visited him last. He was really bad off. He just gave me this note. That's all. During his last moments, he trusted me with whatever secret it represents."

Rebbe Doresh took the note and unfolded it. He then handed it to Mrs. Doresh. Devora walked over and looked at the note over her mother's shoulder. The note read: "UIF NFAAVAB JT UIF USFBTVSF."

"People seem to think we have a treasure in the house," Bracha said. "Maybe there's some secret room or tunnel."

"We had a contractor come down," Mr. Rabinowitz went on. "Someone I trusted. He examined every part of the house, even the *sukkah,* which is attached to the house. He also studied the blueprint of the building. But he could find nothing."

Yankele and Chaim came running into the kitchen

from their play. Mrs. Rabinowitz took one look at Yankele and her mouth flew open.

"Yankele! What happened? Please go into the bathroom and wash up immediately!"

Yankele ran into the bathroom and came back out in less than a minute. His mother's eyebrows raised and Chaim began to laugh.

"Yankele! Don't tell me you washed up already!"

"I did. Really, I did. Look, my hands are still wet!"

"Your hands are also still filthy! Now get back in there and do a better job, young man."

Devora got up and took Bracha by the hand.

"Come on, Bracha, let's take a look at the *sukkah.*"

"I'll be with you in a moment. I just have to say *borey n'foshos.*"[11]

"There isn't much to see," Aunt Baila said. "The *sukkah* hasn't been decorated, yet."

"Don't worry," Mrs. Doresh mused. "Devora's probably interested in investigating the scene of the crime right now."

Bracha rose and the two girls ran out of the kitchen into the *sukkah.* Yankele and Chaim followed them.

"My sister is a detective," Chaim told Yankele. "Have you ever seen a real detective at work?"

"Nope," Yankele replied, staring at Devora. "That's a real detective? Your sister?"

"Yeah. You can tell your friends now that your

11. A blessing said after most snacks.

cousin from Brooklyn is a real detective. Going to *yeshiva*, yet!"

"I didn't know detectives look like that."

"Shhhhhh. I think my sister's discovered something. Look at her eyes. When her eyes get smaller and there are wrinkles on her forehead, it means she's found something."

Yankele walked over to Devora and looked up at his cousin's face. She was standing by the outer door of the *sukkah*, looking at the doorframe. She reached up with her right hand and rubbed it slowly against the upper part of the doorpost.

"What's the matter?" Bracha asked.

"Where's the *mezuzah?* Looks like the *mezuzah* is gone." Devora said softly. Chaim turned to Yankele and smiled.

"Some detective, eh?" He said. Then turning to Devora, he cried: "A *sukkah* doesn't need a *mezuzah*, Devora! Of course there's no *mezuzah* there!"

"Chaim. This is a permanent structure. It's up all year around. Certainly it requires a *mezuzah* like any other room in the house."

"Think it might have fallen off?" Asked Bracha.

"No," said Devora, studying the doorpost. "The *mezuzah* was put up with nails. See the holes here? They were left by small nails. Evidently, someone pried them off."

Chaim and Yankele ran excitedly into the kitchen and summoned both sets of parents. Mr. Rabinowitz walked over to where Devora was standing and looked at the doorpost.

"Fantastic!" he exclaimed. "I never noticed that the *mezuzah* was missing. I didn't for a second think that someone tried to break in to steal a *mezuzah*. Who would think of such a thing? So of course I didn't check it."

"Very strange," Rebbe Doresh said. "Why would anyone want to steal a *mezuzah?* Very strange."

Chaim's face beamed.

"Wait! I know! I know why! The robber was trying to take off the hinges of the door to get in and the *mezuzah* was probably in the way, so he took it off!"

Everyone nodded in agreement and smiled at Chaim's wit. But Devora was unimpressed. "Can't be," she said. "The hinges of the door are on the inside of the *sukkah*. Whoever took off the *mezuzah,* was after just that. A *mezuzah*."

"Maybe there's something secret in the *mezuzos*," suggested Chaim.

"No, no, no," Mr. Rabinowitz said. "I checked the *mezuzos* last week, remember, to see if they were still good and make sure there were no cracks in the lettering and so on. There was nothing at all in those cases that could have meant anything to anyone other than a Jew who understood the meaning of a *mezuzah*. And such a person would certainly not try to *steal* one!"

"Speaking of *mezuzos*," Mrs. Doresh interrupted, trying to change the subject. "We brought some new ones for you as you requested." She handed her key chain to Devora and whispered to her to go fetch the box with the parchments. Devora and Bracha ran through the house towards the front.

"Special *mezuzos,* Shlomo," Rebbe Doresh said. "From Jerusalem, and written by a renowned scribe who is an accepted authority in the writing of *mezuzos* and all the details of the laws relating to it."

"Yes," Shlomo, said. "You have to be extremely careful these days. A lot of invalid *mezuzos* are floating around the market, with labels on them saying they're okay. You have to be careful, you know? You have to check it all out. A lot of people think that if it's made in Israel, it's automatically okay. They don't realize it has to be examined by an authority. There's more than just the need to have complete letters and words. The letters have to be written in a certain way and the scribe must be a truly pious authority on *mezuzos.* Lots of *mezuzos* are printed and sold cheaply. People use them because they don't know the *halachah.*"

"I know," Rebbe Doresh said, nodding his head. Devora and Bracha returned shortly, and Devora gave the box to Aunt Baila. Uncle Shlomo looked at the parchments in his wife's hands and exclaimed: "Big ones. They're very big."

"That's the surest way to be safe," Rebbe Doresh explained. "With smaller ones, it's harder to examine properly to make sure they're valid, and more difficult to repair if they need only a little touch-up a few years later. But most important, the bigger they are, the more likely they were written with all the necessary requirements and proper concentration."

"That's true," Mr. Rabinowitz said. "If the scribe is writing on a small piece of parchment in tiny print, he can barely concentrate or see what he's doing, let alone make sure his intentions are holy."

Just then the bell rang.

"I'll get it!" shouted Bracha. She ran through the living room and opened the door. Turning her head around she yelled: "It's Mr. Mercer!"

Rebbe Doresh and Devora looked at each other in astonishment.

"Mercer?" They both exclaimed at the same time. Mrs. Doresh stopped talking with her sister and looked at her husband.

"Mercer?" She asked. "Who is that? The name sounds so familiar."

"The man in the van," Devora said. "Remember he said he got the order for the sand from a Mr. Mercer?"

"Oh, right. Mr. Mercer."

"You know him?" Baila asked as Uncle Shlomo got up from his chair to go to the door.

"Not really, we just heard about him on the way up here," Mrs. Doresh said. Devora left the kitchen to follow her uncle. Mr. Rabinowitz stood by the door facing a tall, heavy man perspiring heavily. A thick cigar butt wiggled around between his yellow teeth and the excess skin hanging around his jowls shook like jello. Behind him, Devora saw a pretty blue 1979 Cadillac, with a slim chauffeur sitting in the driver's seat.

"Well, well, Mr. Mercer," Mr. Rabinowitz greeted the man. "What brings you here, sir?"

"Who are all these people?" He asked in a hoarse voice. He coughed several times and wiped his forehead.

"These are the relatives I told you we were having for our holiday."

"Oh, yes, the holiday, uh . . . what is it called again?" He coughed again and wiped his lips.

"*Sukkos.*"

"Oh, yeah, right. Yeah. Well, isn't it tomorrow night?"

"Yes, it is, Mr. Mercer, but my brother-in-law's family came up a day earlier so they could help us out with all the preparations."

"Yeah. Yeah, makes sense. But I don't know. I never heard of this holiday. I worked with lots of Jews in my life, in the gold and diamond businesses. I remember there being a holiday called, uh . . . uh Yom . . . uh . . ."

"*Yom Kippur!*" Devora exclaimed.

"Yeah. Yeah, kid, that's right. And then there was another one, called Rash, uh . . . Rashana, something like that."

"*Rosh HaShanah!*" Devora broke in again.

"Yeah, kid. Right. And then Passover.[12] Everyone knows about that one. But the other one, uh . . . suk . . . sukkee . . . uh . . ."

"*Sukkos!*"

"Yeah, right, uh . . . whatever it is, I never heard of it and none of my Jewish friends celebrate it."

"Well," explained Mr. Rabinowitz, "there are a lot of Jews who are unfortunately not familiar with their tradition . . ."

"Yeah, right," interrupted Mr. Mercer. "But, like, I sure was hoping you'd have some room for some of my convention guests. We've got a lot more people at this gold-collector's thing than I had originally expected. The hotel in town is filled up and my house is bursting at the seams. You sure you can't have one or two people sleeping over here two nights?"

"I'm sorry, Mr. Mercer, but, as much as I would like to, I cannot accommodate you. I already explained to you last week that this is a sacred holiday, and my relatives and I wish to celebrate it in its proper spirit without any interruption or distraction. So, again, I'm afraid the answer is no."

Mr. Mercer, looking downcast, shrugged his big shoulders. He was used to getting his own way, and being turned down was something he had not bargained for.

"Yeah," he said. "I guess I understand."

---

12. Jewish holiday of liberation from slavery.

"I mean, you wouldn't feel too thrilled if I were to bother you during your religious holidays with *my* guests. Would you?" Mr. Rabinowitz asked.

Mr. Mercer looked outside at his shiny Cadillac and then back into Mr. Rabinowitz's eyes. "No, I guess I wouldn't." The man was about to leave when Aunt Baila came to the door.

"Oh, Mr. Mercer, how are things?"

"Fine, ma'am. Have a good day. I better get going."

"Oh, by the way," Aunt Baila said. "You didn't get a chance to show that mysterious code to your brother, did you?"

Mr. Mercer's eyes flew wide open. He swallowed hard and started coughing violently, wiping his forehead with his handkerchief. Bracing himself, he cleared his throat several times and smiled at Mrs. Rabinowitz.

"Yes," he said. "Yes, in fact, I did show him that secret code you showed me. And he . . . uh . . . he put it through the computer like I said he would. He called me the other day, I forgot to tell you, and he said it's nothing. No code or anything at all. Probably the old man was so sick he didn't know what he was doing. Probably nothing but meaningless scribble. If I were you, I'd stop thinking about it and throw the note away. It's worthless."

He turned around and walked quickly down the three steps to the lawn. Devora watched him intently as he approached the car. The chauffeur got out of the car and opened the back door for Mr. Mercer, and the big man climbed in. As the car drove off slowly, Devora kept her eyes on it till it pulled up in front of the house near the lake, the house which resembled her uncle's house so much.

"Interesting," Devora said out loud to herself. Uncle Shlomo was still near the door and heard her.

"Who, him?"

"No, the house. His house and your house look like twins."

"Oh, yes, that's right. See, this area was originally developed by a Mr. Fink who came here from Europe before World War Two in the beginning of the Nazi terror in Germany. He was very scared when he came. The Nazi horror was spreading fast throughout Europe and he was afraid they would eventually come to these shores too. So he built himself a house near the lake, the one Mr. Mercer owns now. And in the house, he built some kind of secret room, they say. I haven't seen it, but so I was told by Mr. Hirsch."

"What about your house?"

"Well, it seems Mr. Fink changed his mind about living near the lake and he decided to have a similar house built a distance from the water. He probably felt safer that way. You can imagine the nightmares he lived through before he was able to escape to America."

"So this house must also have a secret room," Bracha suggested. "But we haven't found any."

"I don't understand," Devora contemplated. "Why

does Mr. Mercer want his guests to stay here? There are plenty of other homes around here."

"Could be he thinks they can use the furnace in the cellar to smelt their gold. Mr. Hirsch used it for baking *matzah* when he owned the house. Each house has a furnace in the cellar. But I don't think ours works."

"Think there's a secret passageway in the oven?"

"I checked that out already," Bracha said. "There's nothing in the oven but old charcoal."

"Look, girls," Mr. Rabinowitz said finally. "You're both getting too sophisticated for me. I must help Aunt Baila with the cleaning. And then there's still some work that needs to be done with the *sukkah*. So you two stand here and figure out all the mysteries by yourselves."

He walked away towards the kitchen. Bracha motioned to Devora to follow her. The girls ran up the stairs to Bracha's room.

"My suitcase is here," explained Devora. "I guess this is where I'm sleeping, right?"

"Hey, that's good," Bracha said, jokingly. "You figured that one out, now let's see you solve the mystery of this house."

"Give me some time and I will *b'ezras Hashem*,"[13] Devora said, lifting her suitcase onto one of the beds. "By the way, is Mr. Fink still around?"

---

13. "With G-d's help."

"No one knows where he is. He retired some time ago, but first he sold his two houses, the one by the lake to Mr. Mercer and this one to Mr. Hirsch. If he were around, he could certainly tell us where the secret room is."

"If there is one." Devora said, frowning. She looked around the room. It was much bigger than her own room back in the city. The room had two windows, one large and one small. The small window overlooked the side of the house and it was necessary to stoop over a little to look out of it. The larger window faced the rear of the house where the *sukkah* extended into the back yard.

On the wall near the closet door, Devora noticed a large poster taped securely on the wallpaper. The poster showed animated caricatures of each of the letters in the Hebrew alphabet. The letters seemed to be dancing in a long line in according to their alphabetical order, complete with smiling faces and waving arms.

"I've never seen a poster like that before," Devora remarked, smiling.

"You like it?" Bracha asked. "I made it myself. I planned on giving it to you to take home after *sukkos*. I hung it up so you would see it when you came in."

Devora went over to Bracha and hugged her tight.

"Thanks so much. I do like it. It's very different. But what does it mean? You always draw things that have some corresponding lesson from the Torah. What is it?"

"Well, do you remember the *midrash* about what

was going on in Heaven before the Ten Commandments were given?"

"There is more than one *midrash* on that, which
one?"

"Well, we learned in *yeshiva* that at that time all the
letters of the Hebrew alphabet aspired to be chosen as
the beginning letter of the Ten Commandments. But
the letter *Alef,* the first and silent letter of the alphabet,
did not act with pride and haughtiness. Seeing this, G-d
selected the *Alef* as the first letter of the Ten Commandments, to teach us that G-d favors the humble. So
I drew a picture of all the other letters dancing behind
the *Alef* who is embarrassed by the honor, see?"

Devora smiled and began to chuckle. "That's very
good, Bracha, I really like it. Every time I look at it, I'll
try to remember that if the first letter of the alphabet
could be so humble, so much more should I be."

"Wanna see some of my other drawings?" Bracha
asked. Without waiting for a reply, she opened the top
drawer of her dresser and pulled out a wad of paper.

"Bracha!" Someone shouted from downstairs.

Bracha dropped the drawings on Devora's bed and
ran for the stairs. "My mother probably needs me to
help."

Devora glanced briefly at the drawings and started
to unpack. As she hung the last article of clothing in the
closet, her eyes were attracted to Bracha's painting
again. She felt bad. Her cousin had put her talents to use
to give her a special gift, but she didn't bring anything

for Bracha. Devora made up her mind to use her own special skills to give Bracha the thrill of her childhood by finding the secret passageway. Somehow. If there was one. She sat on the bed and sighed.

Rebbe Doresh called up the stairs for Devora. They were getting ready to perform the *mitzvah* of putting the new *mezuzos* on the doorposts. Devora slammed her empty suitcase shut and slid it underneath her bed. Then she went down the staircase to join the others.

Mr. Rabinowitz was slipping a parchment scroll into a gold encasement. Aunt Baila approached with a hammer and two small nails. Holding the new *mezuzah* to the doorpost, Mr. Rabinowitz slanted it slightly so that the top slanted towards the inside of the room. He stuck one of the nails through the top hole of the *mezuzah* case and began to hammer. Then he recited the appropriate blessing in Hebrew: "Blessed are you, Hashem our G-d, king of the universe, who made us holy through His commandments and commanded us to affix the *mezuzah*." Everyone said *"Ah-meyn"*.

They put up two other *mezuzos* in the kitchen and at the front door. Then the family walked to the *sukkah* to replace the stolen *mezuzah*.

That night, when Devora and Bracha were in bed, they whispered to one another about where the secret passageway or secret room, whichever it might be, would be located.

"It must be in the cellar," Bracha said.

"How do you know?"

"I don't know how I know. I just know, that's all. Where else would someone put a secret room? In the kitchen?"

The girls giggled and continued whispering to one another for more than an hour before they finally fell asleep. Devora dreamt of doors opening and closing. Neon lights flashed on and off above the doors: "secret door, secret door . . ."

Suddenly, she awoke, startled. She had heard a strange hissing noise. It sounded as if it had come from underneath the bed. Devora sat up petrified and kept telling herself it was only in the dream. But as she moved around on the bed, she heard the sound again: "Mashhhhhhh."

She started tapping the bedsheet with her hands, trying to find the cause of the noise. Then she realized that she had been sleeping on her windjacket which still had her mother's key chain in the pocket, along with the whispering *mezuzah*.

Devora smiled in relief and yanked the jacket out from underneath her covers. She draped it over a chair near the bed and tried to go back to sleep. But now she could not stop thinking about the mysterious sound of the *mezuzah*. What did "Mashhhhhhh" mean? What was the *mezuzah* saying? As she was thinking about it, she started dozing off again when suddenly she heard another sound. She sat up again, listening carefully. It sounded as if someone was tampering with a door outside. But since she had been half asleep when she heard the noise, she wondered whether the sound was real or imaginary.

A cricket sang nearby, and a cool breeze blew in through the open window. As Devora's eyes began to get used to the dark, she took in the sight of the room in the eerie silence. Turning her face to the right, she saw the silent form of her cousin, fast alseep, and she told herself again that the sound she had just heard was from within her sleep, not from the house. Otherwise, she figured, Bracha would have heard it, too.

It was a little chilly and Devora's teeth began to chatter. She crawled out of bed and walked quietly to the smaller window to shut it. Standing in the breeze, she took the moment to look into the still of the night and fill her lungs with some fresh country air.

Then she saw a light. She shut her eyes and opened them again, to make sure she was not just seeing things. Down below near the side entrance to the house, a small light was dancing around. She squinted and focused her eyes on a shadowy figure behind the light, crouching by the door. Whoever it was, she could not figure out whether he was trying to get in or out of the house.

"Stop!" she shouted. "Stop! Who's there!"

Bracha sat up in her bed, startled by Devora's sudden yelling.

"What's the matter, Devora?" She croaked, sliding out of her bed. She staggered half asleep to the window and peered out. Devora pointed at the shadowy form

which ran quickly around the house, the flashlight off. Bracha saw nothing through her tired, foggy eyes, but she heard the footsteps of the fleeing man.

Suddenly, the door opened, and Mrs. Rabinowitz entered.

"What's wrong, girls?"

"Devora saw someone trying to break into the house again," Bracha said.

"He tried getting in or out the side door," Devora said. Devora closed the shudders. There was a soft tapping on the door. "Can we come in?" Rebbe Doresh asked. The girls put on their robes. Mrs. Rabinowitz opened the door for the two men. Mrs. Doresh soon joined.

"Looked like he was carrying a flashlight," Devora went on. When I screamed, he ran. Real fast."

Mr. Rabinowitz shook his head from side to side.

"You shouldn't have screamed, Devora. You should have alerted us about it and we would have caught him in the act."

"But I didn't know if he was going in or coming out. I mean, he could have had a gun, you know."

"She's right," Rebbe Doresh interceded. "It's not worth the risk. You did the right thing, Devora. Whoever it was, he was certainly scared away and surely will not think of coming back here again, at least not tonight. Tomorrow, we can contact the police and report it, but right now I can think of nothing wiser than all of us going back to sleep."

Everyone agreed and returned to their rooms.

Early the following morning, the girls got up and dressed. They went downstairs to *daven*[14] and eat breakfast. In the alley way, their fathers were talking with a police officer who leaned against a squad car, taking notes. The two girls walked out to join them.

"This is the person you should be talking to," Mr. Rabinowitz told the officer, pointing to Devora. "She caught the fellow red-handed and scared him away with her screams."

"Good morning, young lady. Do you recall what the intruder looked like?"

"No, officer. I couldn't see anything but his flashlight and his form moving past the apple trees. But he must have been thin."

"What makes you say that?"

"Well, he ran awfully fast. You should have seen him!"

A second policeman approached from the street in front of the house, looking at a shiny object in his hand.

"Hey, Charlie, look at what I found." He said. He handed the object to his partner. It was a *mezuzah*.

"Look!" exclaimed Mr. Rabinowitz, motioning to Rebbe Doresh. Rebbe Doresh moved closer to take a look.

"That's one of ours," said Mr. Rabinowitz. The officer gave it to him.

14. Pray.

"This is probably the one they stole from the *sukkah* two nights ago!" Rebbe Doresh suggested. But Mr. Rabinowitz was not convinced of that.

"Looks a little different. Looks shinier, newer", he said.

The two officers looked at each other, completely puzzled.

"I found it on the grass down the street, towards the lake," he said, squinting in the sunlight. "You know, sometimes these crooks drop things while in flight. Guess that's what he dropped. And it probably got a nice shine lying in the dew all morning."

"What's inside these things anyhow?" the first officer asked.

"A roll of parchment with the biblical commandment of having this on every Jewish doorpost."

"Why, then, would anyone want to steal it?" he asked.

Mr. Rabinowitz looked at Rebbe Doresh who looked at his daughter. But Devora said nothing. The officers then put away their note pads and walked to the side door to search for fingerprints.

"The burglar probably used gloves," Devora muttered to her cousin. "They won't find any fingerprints. Watch."

After several minutes, the officers returned to their squad car.

"Find anything?" Devora asked.

"Nope. No fingerprints or anything," one of the officers said. Devora turned to Bracha and whispered, "See? I told you."

Mr. Rabinowitz leaned over into the window of the car and spoke with the two officers.

"Awfully strange things happening around your house, mister," one of the officers said. "Two nights in a row. Must be something really big these guys are after. Do you have any real valuables in your house?"

"No, officer. I wish I did. At least then I would understand why these characters were trying to break in. But like this—I can't figure it out and it bothers me to no end."

"Well, all I can tell you," the officer said, "is that we'll keep an eye on your house tonight as much as we can during our patrol, and we'll alert the others at the station to make it their business and come around this area several times during the night. And then we'll see what happens."

"Thanks a lot, officer," Mr. Rabinowitz said as he backed away. The car reared itself out of the driveway and back onto the street. Devora stood silent with her cousin and watched the police car drive away, causing a heavy cloud of dust and pebbles to swirl into the air.

"Let's go down," Devora said.

"Down? Down where?"

"Down to the basement. Let's take a look down there and start solving this mystery."

"Well, okay, but we better solve it fast before my mother calls us. Tonight is *Yom Tov*[15] and there's still a lot of work to be done."

"I realize that. But don't you think we would enjoy the holiday more if we'd solve this thing?"

"Yeah. I guess so. Let's go."

The girls walked quickly down the cellar stairs from the alley door. Bracha turned on the light switch and led Devora to the old oven. But Devora's eyes were fixed on the walls around the cellar.

"Wow," Devorah remarked. "This is fascinating."

"What? This old beat-up oven?"

"No. The paintings on the walls. You did them?"

Bracha giggled.

"Of course not, Devora. I couldn't do a job as good as that. They're not really paintings. Mr. Hirsch did them some years back before he sold us the house, I guess. He chiseled the outlines into the wall and then painted them. He once told us how he did it when he was showing us around before we moved in. He said he held a spike and a hammer and hammered the spike into the stone wall. Looks like what they call 'abstract art', doesn't it? I can't make it out. I guess it's just a pretty design, that's all."

Devora walked over to the wall and let her fingers follow the grooved outlines of the design.

"Wait a minute," she said, staring at the outlines.

15. The festival.

"This isn't a picture. These are words. Hebrew words.
Look, Bracha."

She pointed to the outlines and showed Bracha how
the chiseled strokes formed different Hebrew letters in a
very fanciful script.

"Wow," Bracha said, excitedly. "I never realized.
We never noticed that."

"Well, let's piece the letters together." Devora
began to sound off the letters slowly until she was
finally able to read the intended phrase.

"Kozo B'muchsoz Kozo," she read.

"What does that mean?"

"It sounds very familiar. Just a second. Yes. Now I
remember, we learned in *yeshiva* that on the blank side
of some *mezuzos* is written in Hebrew: 'Hashem our
G-d is Hashem.'"

"In Hebrew? Sure doesn't sound like Hebrew to me.
Sounds more like Aramaic or something, doesn't it?"

"Well, I remember the teacher explaining that this is
another way to say Hashem's name. We're taught this
in the *kabala*.[16] See, if you take the letters which appear
before these letters, in the Hebrew alphabetical order,
you'll have the proper Hebrew wording. You just have
to think of which letter comes alphabetically before
each of the letters in 'Kozo B'muchsoz Kozo' and you
have it."

"Hey, that's really interesting. We didn't learn

16. Secret teachings of the Torah.

about that yet in class. I wonder if my father knows about that being written on the wall. I bet he didn't notice it."

"Let's find out. It might help us solve this whole mystery, you know. I just have to figure out how."

The girls walked up the stairs and found their fathers seated together around the dining room table studying the Talmud. Not wishing to disturb them during Torah study, the girls went into the *sukkah* to help their mothers hang up the decorations. Yankele and Chaim were there, getting in everyone's way more than actually helping. But the mothers, nevertheless, realized the importance of encouraging children to help in the preparation of the *sukkah*.

The day was passing quickly. The women busied themselves with the food preparations while the men cleaned up the house. The children worked on the *sukkah,* hanging assorted trimmings from the *s'chach*[17] and taping home-made pictures on the walls. Rebbe Doresh, his left arm in a sling, vacuumed the living room carpet with his right hand while Mr. Rabinowitz ran a mop across the hallway linoleum.

Mr. Rabinowitz passed through the living room to get some more soap.

"Listen," he said to Rebbe Doresh, "you and your wife can sleep in the *sukkah* tonight, because I won't be able to. Remember? I'm just getting over a long

17. Covering for *sukkah* usually made from bamboo poles or cut branches.

battle with a bad cold and sleeping outdoors at this point won't do me any good."

"Are you sure, Shlomo?"

"I'm positive. Doctor's orders. I checked with my physician first because I know it's a great *mitzvah* to sleep in the *sukkah*. Go ahead. I'll set up the beds as soon as I finish with these floors."

"Thank you so much, Shlomo."

A little more than an hour passed and things began to get hectic. *Yom Tov* was approaching fast. The sun was sinking behind the colorful hills on the other side of the lake. Mrs. Rabinowitz rushed back and forth with settings for the table while Mrs. Doresh set up the candelabra in the *sukkah* for the lighting of the candles in honor of the festival.

The rest of the household were getting dressed in their special festival outfits, while some were showering.

"Okay, girls!" shouted Mrs. Rabinowitz. "We're ready to light the candles. Come on down."

Devora and Bracha came quickly into the *sukkah*, Bracha still brushing her hair. The girls took their positions in front of the candles and prepared to recite the proper blessings.

The doorbell rang.

"The men will have to get it," Mrs. Doresh said. "We're running late."

Mrs. Rabinowitz walked briskly to the adjoining kitchen and shouted for her husband to come down and answer the door. Returning to the *sukkah,* she joined the girls in reciting the blessings over the candles.

"Blessed are you, Hashem our G-d, king of the universe, Who made us holy by His commandments and commanded us to light the candles of *Yom Tov.* Blessed are you, Hashem our G-d, king of the universe, who has granted us life and sustained us and allowed us to reach this season."

Mr. Rabinowitz rushed down the stairs into the room, still buttoning his shirt. He did the last button, straightened his collar, and went to the door. Upon opening it, he met a lean, young man with a small beard and a thin mustache. He was neatly dressed, wearing a black suit and hat, and a white shirt.

"Hello," he said, smiling uneasily. "I'm really sorry to disturb you. I need a place to stay for *Yom Tov.*"

"You are very welcome here, my friend," said Mr. Rabinowitz with a broad grin. "Just in time, come on in. Tell us how you happened to be out here just before *Yom Tov.*"

"Why thank you. Very kind of you. My name is Markowitz. I live in Boro Park, Brooklyn. I was travelling on my way upstate for *Yom Tov* when my car broke down. So I left it on the highway and walked to your town here, since it is the nearest to the highway. I asked around whether any Jews live here and was happy to hear that you've got a real growing Jewish community here, with a *yeshivah* and all. The first fellow I asked directed me to your house, Mr. Rabinowitz. I guess you're well-liked here. I can see why."

"Say no more, friend. Just hurry in and get rid of any money or other things you may not carry on the holiday."

"I locked all my valuables in the car. I didn't want to take any chances carrying them with me on *Yom Tov.*"

"Good thinking. Come on in. You can sleep on the high-riser in the living room, right over there. But right now, I suggest you relax for a few minutes and join my brother-in-law and me on our way to *shul.*"[18]

"Fine."

Rebbe Doresh came down the stairs, dressed in his freshly cleaned suit. Mr. Rabinowitz went to the closet in the hallway to get his tie and soon the three men were on their way to *shul,* with Chaim and Yankele running ahead.

The girls sat in the living room, studying *Chumash*[19] together, while Mrs. Doresh and her sister caught up with their *davening.* About an hour later, the men returned and Mrs. Rabinowitz brought the wine and *challahs*[20] out into the *sukkah.* Chaim ran over to Devora, who sat pondering over a difficult *Rashi*[21] with Bracha.

"Devora," he whispered. "That man, Mr. Marko-

18. Synagogue.
19. Five books of the Torah.
20. Traditional bread.
21. A famous Jewish biblical expositor.

witz, from Boro Park is a real *tzadik.*[22] You should have seen him *daven.* His eyes were shut and he was swaying back and forth and shaking his head. He never once looked into a *siddur.*"

"That makes him a *tzadik?*" Bracha asked, smiling at Chaim. "I don't think the criteria for a *tzadik* is how much he shakes when he *davens* or whether he can pray without looking into a *siddur.*"[23]

"Absolutely right," Devora emphasized.

Mrs. Rabinowitz ushered everyone into the *sukkah* and handed the wine bottle to her husband. He poured the wine into the shining silver cup and then turned to Rebbe Doresh.

"We usually make *kiddush* and keep everyone in mind when we have guests," he said. "But if you prefer, I'll get you a cup and you can make *kiddush* for your own family."

"That's okay, Shlomo," Rebbe Doresh said. "Keep us all in mind. We'll be included in your *kiddush.* When you're in someone else's home, it's proper to follow the customs of the host. Go ahead. Make *kiddush* for us all."

"How about you, Mr. Markowitz?" Asked Uncle Shlomo.

"Yes?"

"Would you want to make your own *kiddush?* Or should I keep you in mind?"

---

22. A very righteous Torah observant Jew.
23. Prayerbook.

"Uh . . . yes, keep me in mind. Please. Thanks."

Mr. Rabinowitz recited the *kiddush* slowly, concentrating intensely on every word and its meaning while the two families and the guest stood still, listening. When he completed the *kiddush,* the wine was passed around for all to drink and everyone rose to wash their hands for the *challah.* Mrs. Rabinowitz brought a large basin and some washing cups into the *sukkah* and placed them on the ground near her husband. Mrs. Doresh came with two large pitchers of water. All washed their hands in the *sukkah,* and returned to their seats. Mr. Rabinowitz recited the blessing over the *challahs,* sliced one of them, and distributed the slices to all present.

The meal was a welcome experience for all. For an entire day they had been smelling the tantalizing aroma of the *Yom Tov* delicacies from the kitchen. Everybody enjoyed the meal immensely, experiencing the joy of the festival.

"It's a very special feeling," Mrs. Doresh remarked, looking up at the stars through the *s'chach.* "You really feel that Hashem is watching over you, don't you?"

"That's one of the things we're supposed to experience," Rebbe Doresh explained, chewing on a chicken bone. "We are commemorating *Hashem*'s direct guidance and protection over us during our dangerous 40-year journey through the desert, following our redemption from Egyptian slavery. This is an opportunity to step out of the permanence of our year-round routine and its material security, and to remind our-

selves where our *real* security lies. In *Hashem*. So we
have a temporary roof over our heads, to minimize
symbolically the material protection we experience all
year round and to emphasize the spiritual protection of
Hashem."

Mrs. Rabinowitz placed a dessert dish in front of the
new guest.

"So tell us a little bit about yourself, Mr. Markowitz."

Rebbe Doresh raised his right hand.

"Hold it. Forgot to tell you, Baila. Mr. Markowitz
explained to us that he recently underwent an operation
on his larynx and he must not speak unnecessarily."

"Oh," Mrs. Rabinowitz exclaimed. "I apologize,
Mr. Markowitz. I hope it heals up. A young man like
you. Would you prefer something warm to drink?"

Mr. Markowitz smiled and nodded his head. He
cleared his throat a few times. "Yes," he said hoarsely.
"Thank you, I'll have something warm. I did too much
talking already today when my car broke down and I
wandered through town." He coughed and swallowed.
"Tomorrow," he said, clearing his throat again.
"Tomorrow I should be able to talk better. I'll tell you
all about myself then."

"Good enough," Mrs. Rabinowitz said, as she left
the *sukkah* to get some tea.

After the meal, the family recited the *Birkas Ha-
Mazon,* after which the children headed for bed.

Devora was extremely tired from all the excitement of being with her cousin again after not having seen her for years and from all the baffling mysteries that confronted them in her uncle's house.

"I sleep better with the shutters open," Bracha said. "If you get too cold, Devora, you could put a sweater over your nightgown."

"Good idea. I'll be okay, it's too warm to wear the sweater now."

"By the way," said Bracha, "I'm leaving a baseball bat by our beds in case someone tries to break in again tonight."

"Good idea. I sure hope there's no break-in through the *sukkah,* though, because my mother and father are sleeping there tonight."

"Well, we'll have to sleep with our ears open."

"Yeah. Although, chances are that the *sukkah* will not be broken into after all. I'm sure *Hashem* will take care of that, just as He took care of our ancestors in the open desert."

The girls climbed into their beds. Too tired to talk through the night, they fell asleep quickly. Outside, the leaves began to rustle in the soft autumn breeze, sending a mild gust into the room where the girls slept. Shortly after midnight, the room began to get chilly. Devora squirmed beneath her blanket, curling her legs up so that her knees almost touched her chin. But still the cold breeze reached her and penetrated into her bones.

Finally, she realized that she had to get up from her comfortable and much-needed sleep and put on her sweater.

She sat up lazily on her elbows and waited. Maybe her sweater would come over to where she was, she mused. But to her disappointment, it remained in its place, on the chair near the door. She moved onto the cold floor and made a dash for her sweater. Shivering, she pulled the sweater over her head and headed back toward the bed. In her dash for the sweater, Devora accidentally whisked her windjacket off the chair onto the floor, and now she stepped on it as she made her way across the room. Again, the *mezuzah* on her mother's key ring went 'Mashhhhhh, Mashhhhh." Devora was startled by the sound but reminded herself immediately of the whispering *mezuzah*.

She felt warmer as she crept back into bed but she could not fall back to sleep as fast as she expected to. In her mind, she tried to figure out the meaning of "Mashhh" but to no avail. It felt like an entire hour had gone by and still she could not fall asleep, nor could she figure out the strange message of the whispering *mezuzah*.

She turned on her right side and stared at the outline of the "Alef-Beis" picture which her cousin had made for her. Since she had been awake in the dark for a long time, her eyes grew used to the dark and she was able to barely make out the animated letters on the poster. Devora smiled. The Hebrew letters seemed very much alive, as if they were really dancing in an alphabetical order behind the *alef.*

She was reminded of the story her mother had once told her about the poor Jewish peasant boy who came to *daven* in the *shul* of the *Baal Shem Tov.* The boy did not know how to read the prayerbook. His only knowledge of Hebrew was the recitation of the Hebrew alphabet. With a sincere heart and tears streaming down his face, the boy began to speak to G-d in Russian in a low voice. "Dear G-d," he said, "I can't read Hebrew and I really would like to pray to you in the Holy Language, the language with which you created the world, the language with which you gave us the Torah. All I know is the Hebrew alphabet. I will recite it for you, G-d, but please, you arrange the letters up in Heaven so that they will spell out the prayers in the *siddur.*"

The thought of the story reminded her of the strange arrangement of letters she had encountered *twice* in her uncle's house. Once, when she was shown the mysterious code that Mr. Hirsch had given Uncle Shlomo, and the second time when she had discovered the Hebrew on the basement wall: *Kozo B'Muchsoz Kozo.*

Her heart began to pound wildly and she felt herself perspiring. Maybe the sweater was too warm, she thought. Or, perhaps she was getting an idea. She grew excited all of a sudden and sat up in her bed.

"That's it!" She whispered to herself. Maybe the two codes were related. Maybe the one Mr. Hirsch wrote in English can be figured out the same way, just like *Kozo B'muchsoz Kozo.* The letter preceding each letter in the alphabetical order. That's it! Maybe. She could not remember Mr. Hirsch's code except for the letters "UIF" which she remembered was repeated twice in the note.

"Let's see," she whispered to herself. "The letter before 'U' is 'T.' The letter before 'I' is 'H', and the letter before 'F' is 'E' . . . 'The'. It might work. It might work for the other letters in the code, too!"

She lay back down again. It was going to be more difficult to fall asleep now than before. How could she fall asleep before trying out the formula on Mr. Hirsch's code. She turned from side to side but could not get relaxed.

Then she heard the noise.

"Pop." It went. "Pop." It was very soft. There was a pause of about two minutes before she heard two more "Pops." Her heart beating wildly, she slid slowly out of bed onto the floor and put her slippers on her feet. At first, she did not want to wake up Bracha, who was sleeping so peacefully. And she needed her rest. But on second thought, Bracha would have been disappointed immensely the next day if she learned how she missed the action.

Walking softly across the wooden floor, Devora bent over her cousin and tapped her gently on the shoulder.

"Bracha," she whispered, shaking her cousin's arm.

"It's me, Devora. Wake up. Someone's downstairs."

Bracha sat up, startled. She reached beneath her bed and pulled out the wash basin to wash her hands six times as is prescribed by the *halachah*. Devora returned to her bed and washed her hands also. The two grabbed their baseball bats and walked carefully to the door.

"Pop." The noise went.

"Hear it?" Devora asked.

"Yes. But that could be someone opening a bottle to get a drink or something."

"Oh yeah? I've heard about five or six 'pops'. One after the other. That's an awful lot of soda."

"Wait a second," Bracha whispered as they edged out into the stairwell. "Mr. Markowitz is sleeping in the living room. If anyone broke in, wouldn't he have heard it?"

Devora's eyes opened wide. Her cousin was right. Poor Mr. Markowitz. What if they hit him over the head or something? The girls started walking down the steps, holding their breath, their baseball bats ready for the swing. Unfortunately, Devora stepped on a creaking step. The sudden sound sent the intruder running through the house in fright.

"There he goes!" Devora shouted as she pointed at a dark figure speeding through the hallway from the kitchen into the living room. Mr. Rabinowitz came out of his room and joined the girls.

"What's going on with you two? This is no time for playing baseball . . ."

"Uncle Shlomo! Quick! Get him!"

Mr. Rabinowitz realized immediately what was happening and ran down the stairs past the girls. By the time he reached the front door, the man was gone, leaving the door wide open. He returned to the living room and then stopped to see if Mr. Markowitz was all right.

"Oh no!" he shouted. The girls came down into the dark living room. Mrs. Rabinowitz stood at the top of the stairs rubbing her eyes.

"What in the world is happening down there?" She yelled. She held on to the handrail as she staggered down the steps half asleep. In the living room, she found her husband and the two girls standing by the high-riser.

"What's wrong?" She asked. "Is he all right? Is Mr. Markowitz all right?"

Mr. Rabinowitz looked at his wife and then bit his lower lip.

"Mr. Markowitz is gone, Baila. He ran out of the house."

Devora walked to the doorway between the living room and the kitchen.

"Just as I thought," she said.

"What's that?" Mr. Rabinowitz asked, walking to where she stood.

"The 'pop' sounds. Look. The *mezuzah* is gone. Someone popped out the nails and took it off."

"This one's gone, too," Bracha said from the living

room. She was standing in the doorway between the hallway and the second living room doorpost.

"I hope they didn't go into the *sukkah*." Mrs. Rabinowitz said. She ran through the kitchen to check on the Doreshes. A *mezuzah* was missing from the doorway leading into the *sukkah*. Not wanting to wake up her sister and brother-in-law, Mrs. Rabinowitz returned to the others in the living room.

"They took three *mezuzos*," she said, "Maybe more."

"Why?" Mr. Rabinowitz asked, addressing his question to no one in particular. "I can't understand it. And where is Mr. Markowitz?"

"He's right here!" Someone shouted from the front lawn. Devora looked out the screen door and saw a flashlight approaching. Holding the flashlight was a police officer. Behind him walked a second officer, leading Mr. Markowitz by the arm.

"Good evening, folks," The first officer said. "I'm Charlie. That's my partner Mike, remember? We came here yesterday to check out the burglary attempt?"

"Yes," Mr. Rabinowitz said, smiling in relief at the sight of the policemen. "Welcome. What's happening?"

"Well, like we promised, we sat out here a good part of the night keeping an eye on the house. We used my personal car so no one would recognize us by spotting a police car around. Then, all of a sudden we see this guy running out of the house. Know him?"

Mike brought Mr. Markowitz into the living room and sat him down. He turned on the light switch.

"Don't worry," Mike said. "We'll turn it off before we go. We know a little bit about Jewish holidays."

"That's Mr. Markowitz!" Mr. Rabinowitz said. Behind him, Rebbe Doresh and his wife came in, yawning. Rebbe Doresh stood beside his brother-in-law and stared at Mr. Markowitz.

"He's our guest, officer." Mr. Rabinowitz protested.

"Yeah," Mr. Markowitz spoke up. "I was running after the thief. I heard some noise and saw this figure moving around. So I startled him. He ran out of the house and I chased after him!"

"See?" Mr. Rabinowitz said. "He's not the thief, officer. He's a guest of ours, please release him at once."

The two officers looked at one another and then back at Mr. Markowitz.

"Look, uh . . . Mr. Rabinowitz. We were watching the house the whole time and the only character we saw running out of it was this guy here. At least we'll have to frisk him, see."

"I protest," Mr. Rabinowitz said. "This is a fellow Jewish guest and I . . ." Rebbe Doresh interrupted his brother-in-law and whispered to him in Hebrew, the language of the Talmud. "When you invite a stranger to your home," he whispered, "the Talmud teaches us to honor him like a prince, yet suspect him like a crook."

Mr. Rabinowitz remained silent. The officers

ordered Mr. Markowitz to his feet and began to frisk
him. Mike felt all along Mr. Markowitz's shirt and
when he reached the waist area, he stopped. Charlie
opened the buttons while Mr. Markowitz began to
protest.

"What are you doing? Mr. Rabinowitz! Please stop
them!"

Charlie put his hand into the shirt and withdrew six
mezuzos. He handed them to Mr. Rabinowitz while
Mike took out his handcuffs and slapped them around
the burglar's wrist.

"Oh!" Gasped Mrs. Rabinowitz. Devora went over
to the China closet and opened the drawer to get the
note with the mysterious code. Using the formula of
Kozo B'muchsoz Kozo, she began to read slowly. It
worked. The letters which preceded each letter on the
note in the alphabetical order, spelled out something.

"The Mezuzah is . . . the . . . treasure."

The crook's eyes flew wide open.

"Hey! How did you do that?" He asked, astonished.
"I had to spend four hours playing around with the
computers to decode that thing!"

Mr. Rabinowitz looked into the man's eyes and
began to snarl.

"'Mr. Markowitz', eh? Maybe you're a Mr.
Mercer? Maybe you're Mr. Mercer's younger brother.
We gave your brother a copy of the code because he
said he had a brother in Brooklyn who worked with
computers. You're that brother, aren't you?"

The handcuffed man lowered his head and did not respond. Yankele and Chaim came into the living room, and the embarrassed intruder could not bear to lift his eyes and look at everyone.

"Yeah," he finally said. "I'm John Mercer. I'm from Brooklyn. I live in Boro Park. That's how I knew how to imitate you Jews. My brother Frank and I, we couldn't resist getting our hands on your *mezuzos*. The code Mr. Hirsch gave you, see, I ran it through the computer several times and when I decoded it, we figured the *mezuzos* were real valuable gold."

"You mean the encasement," Rebbe Doresh corrected him.

"Well, whatever. I owe Frank a lot of favors, and he sure wanted these whatever they are, to show off at the convention, and possibly to sell them for high prices after showing them to an expert. I don't think it's real heavy gold, but its value probably lies in its age, I think. That's what we figured. I mean, well, that's what the code says, just like the girl figured it out: 'The Mezuzah Is The Treasure!'"

"Too bad you got yourself caught," Mike said. "The man comes all the way from Brooklyn to commit a burglary and whammo, into the hoosegow."

"Yeah? Well, everything was planned just fine, see. Frank realized he couldn't find an easy way of getting into the house every night. Each night our man would be found out. So I came up with the idea of spending the night here, being I know how to imitate religious

Jews. I would have pulled this thing off just fine if I wouldn't have gone for too many of them. Frank just wanted four more, but I wanted a few for myself, too. So I spent more time popping them off so I could grab as many as I could."

Chaim seemed to wake up all of a sudden and his face beamed.

"*Tofasto m'ruboh,*" he said, "*lo tofasto!*"

"What's that mean?" the officers asked.

"It means," Chaim explained proudly, "If you grab too much, you grab nothing! The Talmud says that!"

Everyone laughed but John Mercer.

"What about the one we found in the grass?" Mike asked.

"Yeah, well, one of Frank's boys dropped it in flight. In case you cops would catch him and search him you'd have no evidence. He dropped it deliberately in a grassy spot, planning to get it later the next day. But you guys got there first."

"We try," Charlie said, smiling.

"It doesn't make sense." Devora said.

"What doesn't?" Bracha asked. Everyone turned their attention to the "detective."

"If the *mezuzah* is the treasure, if these encasements, that is, are very valuable because of their antiquity, why would Mr. Hirsch keep them exposed like this, just sitting there on the doorposts outside and inside the house? That's a pretty big temptation if someone ever discovered their value, or knew about it."

"What are you getting at?" Mike asked. "What else would the note mean?"

"Well, I'm sure it means what it says, but maybe the *mezuzos* on the doorposts aren't really the 'treasure' ones. Maybe there's a real genuine valuable collection of them somewhere in the house, hidden away. *They* are the real treasures. But these crooks didn't think about that."

"The secret room!" Bracha exclaimed excitedly. "Maybe the real ones are in the secret room."

"What secret room?" Charlie asked, scratching his head. John Mercer looked up and looked at Bracha in puzzlement.

"My brother also thought there was some kind of secret room in his house," the burglar blurted out. "That's just rumors from the Fink days. He looked all over the house and his cellar and found nothing. There ain't no secret room, girl. Don't try to make a fool out of me."

"You're already a fool," Mike retorted. "This gal has you figured out already. Shut up and listen."

Devora was thinking to herself as she sat down on the sofa. The words kept repeating themselves in her mind. "The *mezuzah* is the treasure" "The *mezuzah* is the treasure."

"Wait!" she said, turning to her uncle. "Uncle Shlomo, did you ever notice the Hebrew writing on the wall in the cellar?"

"Writing? What writing?"

"The artistic writing Mr. Hirsch chiseled into the wall downstairs."

"I never noticed it as any kind of writing. I thought it was just abstract art, or something."

"Well, yesterday Bracha and I were down and I found that it really was the Hebrew words: 'Kozo B'muchsoz Kozo.'"

"That's what is written on the back of *mezuzos!*" Rebbe Doresh exclaimed.

"Do you think maybe the chiseled writing of those words was for a purpose?" Devora asked. "Like maybe for the purpose of hinting to a *mezuzah?* Maybe to the left of it is a secret door to a secret room, because *mezuzos* are always placed on the right-hand side of the doorway as you enter, right?"

"Hey, Charlie," Mike said, pulling John Mercer to his feet again. "Let's all go down to the basement and check this thing out."

"Roger."

Everyone made their way to the cellar steps. The women waited for the men to pass down the stairs before following. At the foot of the steps, Mike put the light on and assured Mr. Rabinowitz again that he would turn it off when they left. They walked to the wall against which the oven was hooked. Mr. Rabinowitz squinted as his eyes strained to study the chiseled design on the wall.

"Devora's right!" He said. "Look at this."

Charlie took his nightstick and started beating it

along the wall to the left of the artistic words.

"Nothing," he said, backing off to where everyone stood.

"Wait!" shouted Devora. "Look!"

Suddenly the oven rotated and a part of the wall opened. Shining his flashlight into the secret room, Charlie's mouth flew open. The others followed behind and gasped at the vast collection of valuable antique gold artifacts, most of which were *mezuzah* encasements.

John Mercer looked like he was about to cry. Here was the secret room and here were the *real* treasures of which the secret message spoke.

"We'll have to report all of this," Mike said, staring at the shining gold objects which were wrapped in clear plastic. "But I figure the court will probably let you keep it since Mr. Hirsch gave you the note."

Mrs. Rabinowitz felt faint. Mrs. Doresh put her arms around her to comfort her from all the strange experiences that had happened in the middle of the night. *Sukkos* night of all times.

The family climbed the stairs to the living room with the policemen and Mr. Mercer. The bell rang when they reached the top of the stairs. Mike opened it and greeted a man who seemed very familiar to Devora. She looked up at him a little closer. It was the driver of the van they had helped on the road. The man who was delivering sand.

"Hi, Mike," he said. "Good evening, folks. Name's

Greg Sandrow. I'm with the FBI. Hey. You folks are the nice people who helped me on the road two days ago! How are you? What a pleasant surprise to meet up with you again!"

Rebbe Doresh walked over and shook the agent's hand.

"What was an FBI man doing delivering sand, Mr. Sandrow?"

"Oh? Routine. We've been watching Big Frank Mercer for a few months now, you know. Routine. He's supposed to be smuggling gold in from Mexico, Big Frank. We caught him now. Then we got the report on the radio that he'd been getting his big hands on more than Mexican gold, but also Jewish *mezuzos!* I gotta include that in the report, you know. Routine. So I came over. Big Frank's in the van waiting with a couple of other guests. His chauffeur was the one who burglarized you the second time."

"Skinny guy?" Devora blurted.

"Yeah. He's skinny. Why?"

"I knew he had to be to run that fast."

"Oh you're the one who saw him that night, eh?" The agent looked at the adults again and continued. "We are still trying to figure out how Big Frank got wind of the idea of stealing *mezuzos*. We had them checked by our specialists and they're worth no more than three dollars a piece, these encasements. They ain't no antique either."

"Listen, FBI man," Charlie interrupted. "We think

you're a little too late. This young lady here has already solved the entire mess. We'll tell you all about it as soon as we finish making out *our* report. Now let's all get out of here and stop bothering these people. It's their religious holiday."

Mike escorted John Mercer out of the house while Charlie turned off the living room light. Agent Sandrow went over to Rebbe Doresh and shook his hands again.

"You know, Rabbi," he said, "I'll let you in on a little secret, see. That guy they're taking away, he's really Frank Mercer's brother."

"We know," Rebbe Doresh said, smiling.

"Oh, so you know that, too, eh? I suppose you'll also tell me that you folks captured him, too, eh?"

"Almost," smiled Rebbe Doresh. He looked at Devora. "My daughter caught him in the act and scared him off."

The agent's eyebrows flew up and he looked down at Devora, who was yawning.

"What kept *you* on the alert tonight?" he asked her.

Devora smiled and restrained herself from laughing. "Uh . . . a *mezuzah.*"

"Oh?" the agent exclaimed, his eyebrows raising again.

"My mother has a whispering *mezuzah* and . . ."

"A whispering *mezuzah,* aye? Wait till they hear this at headquarters. And what did this . . . uh whispering *mezuzah* tell you?"

"It went, 'Mashhhhhh, Mashhhhh.'"

Mrs. Doresh broke in.

"You mean you figured it out, Devora?" she asked.

"Well, I think so. It just hit me a few moments ago. I've been thinking about the sound for so long that I kept repeating it in my mind. And if you repeat 'Mashhh Mashhh' long enough, you hear 'Shma, Shma.'"

The agent's eyebrows remained raised and he swallowed hard.

"I think you folks better be getting some rest. Maybe you'll all be okay in the morning."

Everyone laughed.

"'Shma' means 'Hear'," Devora explained. "The *mezuzah* is the Jew's symbol of G-d's protection over him. This little one was trying to make me listen. Its strange message kept me up long enough to hear the intruder."

"Boy," the agent said. "That's lucky. Real lucky, you know?" He waved at the families and walked to the door. As he opened the screen door to leave, he turned around and smiled at Rebbe Doresh, who stood near the doorway staring at him.

"Okay, Rabbi, you win," he said. "Thank G-d, right?"

Rebbe Doresh nodded and smiled.

THE GOLD BUG

ebbe Doresh was about to leave his seat in the *shul*[1] and start for home. The congregation had finished *maariv*[2] ten minutes ago, but Rebbe Doresh always spent several moments studying Torah after services. As he rose to leave, he noticed two strangers standing by the door in the rear of the *shul*. One was a tall man in a freshly cleaned grey suit who could have passed for Sergeant O'Malley. The other was slightly shorter, wearing very thick glasses. Both seemed to be watching Rebbe Doresh as he walked down the aisle to the door.

"Good evening," Rebbe Doresh volunteered as he approached the men. The tall man looked at him in a puzzled way and shook his hand.

"Hi, Rabbi," the man said. "Don't you recognize me?"

Rebbe Doresh took a second look at the tall gentleman.

"Sergeant O'Malley?" he asked, almost in a whisper.

1. Synagogue.
2. Evening prayer.

"Yeah. It's me. Do I look that different out of uniform?" The three laughed together. O'Malley removed the *yarmulke*[3] from his head and ushered the other two out of the sanctuary and into the lobby. He then introduced Rebbe Doresh to the other man.

"Rabbi Doresh, I'd like you to meet Dr. Sax. Dr. Sax, I want you to meet the man I've been bragging to you about, Rabbi Doresh."

The two shook hands, but Rebbe Doresh was still puzzled by the whole scene. What was O'Malley doing in *shul,* and in such a fancy suit? And who was Dr. Sax?

"Now you're probably wondering," O'Malley said, "what I'm doing here in the synagogue, and in such a fancy suit. And you're probably curious to know why I'm introducing Dr. Sax to you."

"Yes," said Rebbe Doresh, "I meant to ask."

"Well, let's all get into my car and drive home where we can enjoy some privacy," O'Malley suggested.

"Home?" Rebbe Doresh asked. "Whose home are you referring to, Sergeant? I promised my wife I'd be right . . ."

"Ah!" O'Malley interrupted. "Your home, of course. That is . . . uh . . . I hope you don't mind, do you?"

"Not at all, Sergeant. But next time I would appreciate a little advance notice."

3. Skull cap, worn by male Jews, who must always keep their heads covered in prayer and during their daily activities.

The three got into a small Ford parked in front of the *shul* and Sergeant O'Malley drove to the Doresh home. When they pulled up in front of the house, O'Malley got out first and looked all around the area as if he was making certain the coast was clear. He then motioned to Dr. Sax and Rebbe Doresh who stepped out onto the sidewalk.

Devora greeted them at the door.

"Abba! Oh! Company! I'll run and tell mommy."

Before Rebbe Doresh could say another word, Devora disappeared into the kitchen. Chaim was seated in the dining room struggling over some arithmetic homework. Seeing his father, he leaped from the chair.

"Abba! Oh! We have company! I'll go tell mommy!"

Mrs. Doresh emerged from the kitchen and greeted her husband and his visitors. She moved toward Rebbe Doresh and whispered to him, "Should I bring the tall one a *yarmulke?*" Rebbe Doresh smiled and nodded "No."

"This is Dr. Sax, everybody," he said, pu   his hand on the man's shoulder. "And this," he continued, pointing toward Sergeant O'Malley, "is . . ."

"Sergeant O'Malley!" Devora shouted.

"Shucks," the officer said, "I thought that just this once I'd be able to fool you, too."

Everyone chuckled. Mrs. Doresh led the group into the living room and flicked on a few light switches. O'Malley and Dr. Sax sat on the sofa while Rebbe and

Mrs. Doresh took their seats in the two armchairs across the room.

Tilting his head from one side to the other and squinting his eyes, Chaim walked cautiously over to Dr. Sax.

"Chaim," Mrs. Doresh called. "What are you doing? Go back to your homework."

Mrs. Doresh got up and took Chaim by the hand, escorting him back to his homework in the dining room. Returning to the living room, she motioned to Devora to leave the room also.

"Wait!" O'Malley protested. "We need Devora here."

"Okay, Devora," Mrs. Doresh said. "Find a seat."

Devora grabbed a chair from the dining room and placed it between the two chairs where her parents were sitting.

"Okay," O'Malley began. "I guess we can get on with it. Folks, this is Dr. Sax. But not really. He is a very special scientist commissioned by our government for top-top secret experiments. So as far as you're concerned, his name is Dr. Sax. I'm on special duty keeping an eye on him, what you'd call 'body guard' while he's here in town. And he's here in town because he is a religious Jew and has to recite the . . . uh . . . the . . . uh . . ."

"*Kaddish,*"[4] Dr. Sax said.

---

4. A special prayer recited by mourners on the anniversary of the passing away of a close kin.

"Yeah, uh . . . right, the *kaddish*. So . . . uh . . . since there ain't no synagogue where he's conducting his experiments, or a . . . uh . . . you know . . . uh . . ."

"*Minyan*,[5]" Dr. Sax interrupted again, smiling behind his thick-lense glasses.

"Yeah, right, uh . . . a *minyan*, so therefore he requested to come into town for tonight's service and he'll be back again tomorrow morning."

Mrs. Doresh left her seat to get some drinks and fruit.

"That's fascinating," Rebbe Doresh remarked. "Very fascinating. We are honored to be able to meet you, Dr. Sax. Very interesting. But why were you assigned to take care of Dr. Sax, Sergeant? Don't they have special agents?"

"Oh, yeah, sure they do. But I know this part of town well and I'm most familiar with the Jewish community here. But besides all that, I bet you never knew I once worked for the Federal Bureau of Investigation (FBI), eh? Well, I did. Except the pay was bad when I was with the Bureau, and the wife and I decided to leave and join the police force. But the FBI people always kept in touch with me, using my services once in a while for special missions, like this one. So they borrowed me from the precinct for about two days."

Dr. Sax cleared his throat. Mrs. Doresh came back and placed a tray of drinks and fruit on the coffee table.

---

5. A gathering of ten males required for saying certain prayers, such as the *kaddish*.

Dr. Sax reached for an apple and made a *bracha*.[6] The Doresh's waited for him to complete the *bracha* and then responded with *"Ameyn."*

"It's the *yahrzeit*[7] of my dear mother, tonight and tomorrow," he said. "So I'll be returning in the morning and then again in the afternoon for *mincha*.[8] But while I'm in town, I'd like to try a puzzle on the young lady."

Sergeant O'Malley took over.

"Uh . . . yeah, I hope you don't mind, but I told Dr. Sax all about Devora and her special skills at solving mysteries. Dr. Sax has a very serious problem. In fact the American government is involved in the problem. The agencies who are trying to solve the mystery are still working at it. Dr. Sax figured that since he was in town anyway, why not try out Devora?"

Devora blushed while her parents eyed her proudly.

Dr. Sax began his story: "I am presently working on a series of very top-secret experiments which will determine somewhat the future direction of our country's defense. We are a small team of four scientists working closely together in a secluded base not far from here. We've moved several times to different locations for security reasons, but still security seems to be our greatest problem. Somehow, the Russians have been

6. Blessing.
7. Anniversary.
8. Afternoon prayer.

getting hold of our formulas and the secret results of our experiments each time. This has been going on for about a year now. American agents in Russia keep reporting to us again and again that the Russians are coming out with the same findings we are working on, alike in every detail. So it is certainly an inside job. One of my colleagues, I'm sorry to say, is feeding information to the Communists."

Devora was about to ask a question, but Dr. Sax had not finished speaking.

"What's worse," he continued, "is that I may soon become the prime suspect in this case."

Rebbe and Mrs. Doresh looked at each other in shock. Even Devora could not refrain from showing puzzlement.

"Why would they suspect you?" Asked Rebbe Doresh.

"Well, because I'm in charge of the entire experiment. But more than that, I'm the only individual on the base who knows the results of the experiments. Not even my colleagues are informed of the results. They are specialists in different scientific fields, Dr. Hall is the Agronomist, Dr. Chin is the Physicist and Dr. Zobel is the Astronomer. Under my direction, they perform specific experiments, but I am the only one who finalizes their results and develops the final formula. Then I transmit the information personally to the Pentagon."

"How do you transmit the secret information?" Devora asked.

"By tape. I record it on a tape recorder and the tape is sent by special courier to Washington."

"Why by tape?" Asked Rebbe Doresh. "Why not by radio in secret codes, or some other ways?"

"Well, codes are practically useless these days with special computers being developed to decode almost anything. If we were to transmit by radio, it would easily be intercepted. If we sent it in writing, it could be stolen in an ambush. We read about armored bank trucks being hijacked these days, you know. But the taping that I do is fool-proof."

"How's that?" Devora asked.

"First of all, it is done in a sound-proof room within a room. There is only one door and it is heavily guarded by armed soldiers. The door is locked by a special combination lock and so is the tape recorder which I use. The combinations for both locks is unknown to anyone but myself and the Pentagon."

"But why couldn't someone steal the tape after you did the recording?" Devora asked. "In an ambush or something."

"It would do them no good. The tape is specially designed to be played only on a machine which sits in the Pentagon. Even *my* tape recorder cannot play the tape back. The only machine which can play it back is sitting in a vault in Washington, D.C. The government is the only agency able to listen to it. So, I simply enter this room and record the results of the experiment of each project and send the tape away to Washington."

"Is there some way," Devora suggested, "that you might have been bugged? that someone might have planted a tiny microphone on your clothes or somewhere?"

"No way. If that had happened at any time, it would have been detected by an 'electric eye' which I pass upon entering the recording room. This 'eye' will pick up anything made of metal or the like." Dr. Sax began to chuckle. "The only thing it ever picked up was my gold bridgework."

Everyone laughed.

O'Malley tapped the professor on the arm.

"Hey, doc, maybe it would help Devora if you'd tell her what you can about the other three scientists working with you."

"Oh, yes, good idea." Dr. Sax said. He removed his glasses and rubbed his eyes. It had been a long day for him, the lab work, the trip into the city, and the pressing need to solve a serious crime in which he was being implicated.

"Well, there's Dr. Hall, a good Agronomist, brilliant man, friendly, but something of a loner. He's helped me out a great deal in the past. His brother's a scientist, too, in Walter Reed hospital. A third brother is a dental surgeon there. In fact, he did extensive capping work on my teeth with gold-backed bridgework. Dr. Hall is a real patriot and is very upset about what's been happening. Last month, he ordered the security increased around the base and spent a good many hours with me, trying to help me solve this mess."

Dr. Sax reached for a glass of orange juice which stood on the coffee table. He made a *bracha* and drank several swallows before continuing.

"Then there's Dr. Chin, originally from Red China. He grew up in a Communist way of life and in his college years, he fled to this country. He likes it here a lot. He's been in the United States now for about eleven years and has worked on very heavy experiments in the past, for our military. A nice fellow, Dr. Chin, very philosophical. I could talk to him about everything, even Judaism. He's a very open-minded person and extremely helpful and cooperative. Extremely handy, too. He once built a wristwatch. About a year ago, when we first got started, Dr. Hall helped Dr. Chin get the assignment and Chin was so grateful to Dr. Hall that he gave him a wristwatch he himself had made, with a tiny built-in transistor radio! Not only that, but at Dr. Hall's request, he tuned it so sensitive that it was able to pick up Dr. Hall's home station in Bowie, Maryland. Isn't that fantastic?"

"Sounds like a very skillful scientist," remarked Rebbe Doresh. Mrs. Doresh nodded in agreement.

"Can he fix washing machines, too?" Mrs. Doresh joked.

Everyone laughed. But Devora sat still, biting on her lower lip. She had been listening attentively to every detail Dr. Sax described. Her suspicion kept jumping wildly from one scientist to the other and the mystery was becoming increasingly difficult.

"Isn't there one more scientist?" Devora asked.

"Oh, yes, Dr. Zobel. He's the Astronomer. One of our country's best, too. He's Jewish, the only other Jew on our base besides me. But he doesn't believe in G-d. You see, he lost his family to Hitler in World War Two. He spent three years in concentration camps and lived through daily horror. After that, he lost his belief in G-d."

Dr. Sax reached for the orange juice again and took a few more swallows before continuing.

"I, too, went through the holocaust."

"You are originally from Europe?" Rebbe Doresh asked.

"Yes. I was born in Poland, in Lublin. The war broke out when I was in my teens and I witnessed my parents and my brother and sister being murdered by the Nazis. But I didn't lose my belief in G-d because of it. I guess everyone reacts to tragedy differently. In fact, my faith in G-d was strengthened rather than weakened. And every time I look around at Jewish communities all over the world today, my faith grows stronger. For thousands of years, our enemies have tried so hard to wipe us out. Many of these nations now exist only in museums and history books. And we're still here."

Rebbe Doresh nodded his head.

"This shows G-d's presence in the destiny of the Jewish people," remarked Rebbe Doresh. "From our first tragedy, our slavery in Egypt some 3,000 years ago, G-d showed that He was with us then, too. The Torah tells us that as hard as they beat us with their whips in Egypt, the more we increased in our population throughout Egypt."

"Is there anything else you can tell us about Dr. Zobel?" Asked Devora.

"Not much else. He's a good man. His reports are well written. He is responsible and very hard working. Like Dr. Hall, he keeps pretty much to himself, but we all do that to some extent, especially after a whole day of watching the sky, peering through a microscope or playing around with mathematical formulas. It's a tough mystery to solve, I admit. I would hate to think that any one of my colleagues would be involved in this crime of treason. But on the other hand, how else could this whole thing be happening?"

O'Malley looked at his watch and stood up.

"Okay, folks, Dr. Sax and I are due back at the lab soon. It's a long drive. He has to get his sleep and I'm sure you all could use a good night's sleep as well. Especially Devora, if she's going to try and solve this crazy mystery. But I must ask you all to please not tell anyone about any of this. I knew I could trust you people and the chief gave me permission to come here so Devora could have a crack at it, because the justice department has been trying to crack this thing a little over a month. Unsuccessfully."

Dr. Sax rose and put his hat on. Rebbe Doresh

recited *borey nefoshos*[9] out loud, thereby reminding Dr. Sax to say it, too. Dr. Sax sat down again and said the brief prayer thanking G-d for the snacks. He then rose and thanked Mrs. Doresh for the hospitality. Both men shook hands with Rebbe Doresh and headed for the door.

"I'll be in *shul* again tomorrow morning," Dr. Sax said to Rebbe Doresh. "I'll see you then?"

"*Im-yertzeh-Hashem,*" Rebbe Doresh said, smiling.

"You always say that," O'Malley said, "What's it mean?"

"It means 'G-d-willing.' "

"Oh. Right. Well, have a pleasant evening and thanks for everything." The two men left the house and walked to the Ford. O'Malley kept looking around. Before he let Dr. Sax into the car, he inspected the back seat.

That night, Devora lay in bed, tossing and turning. The mystery thrown at her that evening was becoming more complicated the more she thought about it. If Dr. Sax was doing his recordings of the secret formulas in a sound-proof room and if he was the only one who knew the results of the experiments, how could the secrets be leaked out? And who, she thought, was suspect from among his fellow scientists? Was it Dr. Hall? Dr. Chin? Dr. Zobel?

It could not be Dr. Zobel, she felt. How would he

9. Blessing recited after eating certain foods.

bring himself to hand over secrets to a country in which almost everyone is a prisoner? Dr. Zobel had been a prisoner himself, under the cruel hands of the Nazis thirty-five years ago. Would he betray the country which gives him freedom to help a country in which no one is free? Nonsense.

Dr. Hall, too, was an unlikely suspect, Devora thought. After all, he has two brothers who are also working for the government, and he even demanded that the security around the base be increased.

That left Dr. Chin. Dr. Chin was born and raised in a Communist country. His escape to the United States eleven years ago could easily have been part of a plot to plant himself in government projects. But, then again, Russia and China were not friendly to one another at all. Why would a Chinaman send secrets to the Russians?

And, most baffling, how was it done?

Devora turned on her left side and shook her head to empty her mind of all her thinking. She wanted to sleep. Tomorrow was *yeshiva*. Tomorrow was also *Rosh Chodesh*[10] and Morah Hartman was surely going to quiz the class on the different things she had taught them about *Rosh Chodesh* during the year.

"We may have used 'smoke signals' before the Indians did," she remembered Morah Hartman saying several weeks before. "In ancient times, the Jews used to

10. Beginning of the new month according to the Jewish calendar (lunar).

send each other signals to announce the coming of the New Moon. When the sages would observe the moon entering its first phase again, at the beginning of the month, they would light a huge bonfire on top of a tall mountain. When the Jews waiting on top of a nearby mountain saw the fire, they, too, immediately lit a bonfire, to alert other observers atop distant hills and mountains. That's how the advent of the New Moon was signalled throughout the Land of Israel."

Devora opened her eyes and looked into the dark. Now she really couldn't fall asleep. Morah· Hartman had given her a clue to the mystery, she felt. Signals. Somehow, as Dr. Sax would speak into his special recorder, his voice was being transmitted elsewhere. But how? If he were walking around with a tiny microphone on his person, the "electric eye" would have detected it as he walked into the recording room. The only thing the "eye" had ever picked up, Dr. Sax had told her, was his gold bridgework.

Devora shut her eyes and turned on her left side. The gold bridgework, she thought. Maybe, inside the gold caps sat a tiny microphone. And as Dr. Sax spoke, it transmitted what he was saying to a radio or something. But how could the microphone have gotten into the gold caps? The caps were put in by government dentists in Walter Reed Hospital, a military hospital in Washington, D.C.! And it was put in by Dr. Hall's brother, yet!

Dr. Hall's brother. Dr. Hall. Dr. Hall's watch.

Devora's mind spun wildly with clues atop clues which were slowly piecing together. That's it, she thought. Dr. Hall and his dentist brother were involved. The microphone was implanted in Dr. Sax's extensive bridgework when it was put on. Dr. Hall then picked up and transmitted the secrets to a distant radio receiver by way of his transistor-radio wristwatch! Why else would he have asked Dr. Chin to tune his radio-watch so he could pick up his home station? His home station was probably not a commercial station but the spy station! Anyone who received such a precious gift would not have asked for more, like Dr. Hall did.

Devora leaped out of bed and turned on the lamp sitting on her desk. She quickly wrote down her theories and jumped back into bed. Dr. Sax would be back in the morning. She would tell him her theories over breakfast.

The following morning, after a tired Devora finished her *davening,* she came down the stairs for breakfast and Dr. Sax was already seated in the kitchen with Sergeant O'Malley and Rebbe Doresh. Devora sat next to her father and recited a *bracha* over the grapefruit juice her mother had prepared for her.

"Well, here's our great detective," O'Malley mused. "Good morning, Devora. Looks like you've been up half the night trying to figure out our latest mystery."

Rebbe Doresh and Dr. Sax smiled.

"Almost," Devora whispered between swallows.

She rose slowly from her seat and reached into the cabinet overhead for a box of cereal. She prepared her own breakfast and sat down again.

"Well, Devora," Dr. Sax said. "What have you got for us?"

"Dr. Sax," Devora began. "You kept saying 'about a year ago.' Everything seems to have happened a year ago. Why?"

"That's when we first got together on these experiments as a team."

"That's interesting," Devora continued. "The leaks began about a year ago, you said. And you had your gold tooth put in about a year ago. And Dr. Chin made his special wristwatch for Dr. Hall about a year ago."

"That's correct, young lady, but all those facts are totally unrelated, I mean, I don't understand what you're getting at."

Devora stood up and began pacing the floor, scratching her chin as she walked.

"There is no way," she continued, "that the secrets could possibly have leaked unless someone had planted a tiny microphone on you. And then, as you would speak into your special recorder in the sound-proof room, the planted microphone would pick up everything you were saying."

Dr. Sax laughed.

"Devora," he said, "you're trying real hard. Maybe you should sleep on it some more, eh?" He winked an eye at O'Malley. "As I said before, Devora, I couldn't have been bugged. The electric eye would have picked it up right away."

"It did," Devora exclaimed, stopping in her walk across the room. Everyone was puzzled by her conclusion.

"Devora," Rebbe Doresh said, "what are you talking about?"

"The gold caps, Abba." She then turned to Dr. Sax. "Your gold-capped bridgework, Dr. Sax. You said it was put in by Dr. Hall's brother in Washington, D.C., right?"

"Yes, but so what?"

"And about the same time, Dr. Chin gave Dr. Hall the special watch, right?"

"Yes, but what has all that to do with it?"

"Well, why would Dr. Hall want Dr. Chin to tune the wristwatch-radio to pick up a radio station in Bowie?"

"Because that's where Dr. Hall lives. That's why."

"Maybe it was so he could transmit your secret formulas through his watch to an enemy spy station where he lived?"

"You mean in my gold teeth sits a tiny microphone?" Dr. Sax asked, half smiling and half annoyed. "Ridiculous. I mean, that's silly, Devora. Come on. You can do better than that. And the wristwatch was a transmitter? Hahahaha. You should write books, spy novels especially. You'd be good at it, right Sergeant?"

But Sergeant O'Malley had learned long ago to take Devora seriously.

"Well, Dr. Sax," he said. "You . . . uh . . . you wouldn't mind, sir, if we stopped off at FBI headquarters on the way back to your base."

"What in the world for?"

"So they . . . uh . . . so they could check out the . . . uh . . . the teeth."

"What?" Dr. Sax exclaimed, growing annoyed. "You, too?"

"It can't hurt, Dr. Sax," Mrs. Doresh said. "I mean, what Devora has said does seem to fit together the more I think about it."

Rebbe Doresh nodded in agreement.

Dr. Sax recited *Birkas HaMazon* with Rebbe Doresh and then stood up, placing both his hands on his forehead.

"Well," he exclaimed. "Looks as though I'm outnumbered. Either you're all looney, or I'm not being sensible. Or both. He smiled at Devora. "I'll give your theory a chance, Devora, but, again, don't get your hopes up too high. And as I said before, you have some good ideas for a spy novel. Why don't you write one?"

He turned to Mrs. Doresh and asked her where she put his hat and coat. Mrs. Doresh left the kitchen to get them. When she returned, O'Malley was thanking Devora for the clues and promised her he would check out every detail of her theory. The two men then shook hands with Rebbe Doresh and departed, walking briskly to the waiting car.

The car took off down the street in the direction of the downtown area. O'Malley headed right for the local FBI headquarters and parked inside the official garage. As he stepped out of the car with Dr. Sax, a policeman approached him and asked for identification. O'Malley removed his wallet from his jacket and flipped it open to show his badge.

"Go ahead, Sergeant," the officer said, stepping aside.

Sergeant O'Malley and Dr. Sax walked through the garage to an elevator. The elevator took them up four flights and stopped. The two then walked down a long, brightly lit hallway and entered a busy office at the other end.

"O'Malley!" one of the agents in the office called. He got up from his desk and walked quickly to the two men. "What in the world are you two doing here? Isn't Dr. Sax supposed to be back on base? It's late."

Sergeant O'Malley set up a folding chair for the professor and motioned to him to be seated. He then turned to the other agent who was now surrounded by others in the office.

"Look guys," O'Malley began, "we have to do a check on Dr. Sax's . . . uh . . . well, on his teeth."

The agents looked at each other and then back at O'Malley. A stocky fellow elbowed his way through the gathering and stood before O'Malley with his hands folded across his chest.

"Oh . . . uh . . . hi, Captain." O'Malley said, a little uneasily.

"Good morning, Sergeant O'Malley. What's going on?"

"Oh . . . uh . . . nothing really, sir. I just stopped by with Dr. Sax to . . . uh . . . well, to examine his teeth, sir."

Dr. Sax cupped his hand over his mouth and started chuckling as everyone stared at O'Malley in puzzlement.

"Sergeant," the officer said, his face showing impatience. "I assigned you to be Dr. Sax's bodyguard! Not his dentist!"

Dr. Sax rose and approached the captain.

"Please, Captain, relax," he said, smiling, "you see, there is a theory going around our private little circle that there is a tiny microphone planted in my gold teeth. We'll never know whether the theory is true unless we check it out."

"A microphone in your teeth?" The captain shouted. "I think there's a record player in both your heads! Professor, in order for anyone to plant anything in your gold teeth, you would have to be aware of it. The only one who ever climbed into your mouth was your dentist. Now, do you suspect him?"

"Captain. Right now, the most trustworthy individuals are under suspicion. Including myself."

The captain lit a cigar and began chewing on it. He walked back and forth with his hands on his hips. Then, he suddenly swung around and waved at Dr. Sax.

"Okay, professor, come on into the laboratory and we'll check it out."

The agents stepped aside to let O'Malley and Dr. Sax pass through to the small laboratory in the rear of the office.

"Chad!" The captain shouted. "Get in here, Chad, we're gonna need a technical wise-guy."

A tall, slim agent with glasses got up from behind a desk and walked casually toward the laboratory. The captain helped Dr. Sax onto a raised leather chair with two armrests. Chad flicked on a powerful overhead lamp and asked Dr. Sax to open his mouth wide. He then walked over to a nearby table with radio equipment and pulled at some extending wires attached to a transmitter, until the wires stretched all the way to where Dr. Sax was seated. He attached a small clamp to the other end of the wires and attached the wires to the gold teeth in Dr. Sax's mouth.

"Don't worry, doc," he said, patting the professor on the shoulder. "This ain't gonna hoit none."

Chad sat down at the table and flicked on a switch on the transmitter. He turned a couple of dials and put a headphone over his ears. The needles on all the dials on the transmitter began jumping wildly and Chad removed the headphones.

"Hey, Captain." Chad exclaimed, getting up. "This

guy's teeth sure got a strong mike in it. Very high powered, too. Seems to be tuned to a certain frequency to transmit a long distance."

O'Malley cleared his throat.

"Yes, sir," he said, smiling at the surprised captain. "Devora's theory was that it transmitted to Bowie, Maryland."

"You mean," the captain asked, "they can hear us talking right now."

"No way," Chad explained. "They would need a transmitter at least within the immediate area in order to do it."

"O'Malley," the captain called. "What's the rest of the theory?"

"Well, according to Devora," O'Malley began. "There's a . . ."

The captain raised his hands to stop the sergeant.

"Wait, O'Malley, who's this 'Devora' you keep mentioning?"

"Oh, well, she's a . . . uh . . . a detective, sir, kind of helping us out on the case."

"She ain't with the police department, is she? This is an FBI case, you know."

"Oh, no, sir. She's not with the police at all. She's a friend and sort of a private detective."

"Good. We'll see how her theory works out in its other details. Chad, take notes. O'Malley, shoot."

The sergeant began explaining Devora's entire theory about the wristwatch transmitter, which probably transmitted Dr. Sax's secret formulas each time he would record them in the special room. He told about the great probability that the traitor was Dr. Hall, and that the secrets were transmitted through his watch to a spy station in his home town, Bowie, Maryland. The captain got on the phone immediately and alerted the FBI in Washington, D.C.

Dr. Sax was returned to the laboratory base where he worked and was instructed to continue his experiments as if nothing had been discovered. Meanwhile, Washington FBI agents set up several high frequency transmitters and other radio equipment near the base and around Bowie. Other agents were assigned to the laboratory base as security guards, with special instructions to watch Dr. Hall's activities when Dr. Sax entered the sound-proof room to record his formulas.

Sure enough, as Dr. Sax locked the door behind him in the recording room, Dr. Hall, strolling outside, did something with his watch and remained standing in the immediate area. The agents on the base called in their observations to their field commander while the agents in the field picked up the "make-believe" secrets which Dr. Sax was recording. They followed the transmission of the recording to a barn near the town of Bowie.

No time was lost.

The FBI field commander opened his own walkie-talkie to all his troops and shouted, "Okay, everyone, move in!" Almost simultaneously, at the laboratory base, two agents walked casually over to Dr. Hall and handcuffed him. Agents stationed near Bowie, drove their jeeps into the farm and surrounded the barn. Hearing the noise of jeep engines, four men ran from the barn and one of them threw a grenade into the barn to destroy all the evidence. The agents moved in and captured the Communist spies at gun point. One of the men captured was Dr. Hall's dentist brother.

The grenade failed to explode, but the agents were afraid to go inside just in case it would suddenly do so. They called in demolition experts who arrived within fifteen minutes by helicopter. The experts wearing heavily padded equipment, walked cautiously into the barn. They found the grenade with the use of a mine sweeper and took it out of the barn gently. The other agents then moved in and took photographs of the radio equipment before removing it for the long ride to headquarters.

Dr. Sax dismissed the laboratory crew for the weekend and called Sergeant O'Malley to pick him up.

"Where do you want to go, doc?" O'Malley asked.

"Into town for the Sabbath. I'll go to a hotel to rest up after all this excitement. And more important, I must thank the Doresh family for everything they did for me and especially Devora."

"Doc," O'Malley said. "I bet if the Doreshes hear about what you plan to do, they'll demand you stay with them for the Sabbath. That's the kind of people they are."

O'Malley picked up Dr. Sax and drove him back to the city.

"Sergeant," Dr. Sax suddenly said. "Listen. Let's just stop off at the Doreshes to thank them."

"Okay with me. I wish you could have been there last night, when I called Devora and told her that her theory proved correct. I wish I could have been there."

"Did the captain meet her, yet?" Asked Dr. Sax.

"I don't think so. He said something about thanking her in person before the weekend. I gave him her address."

The car pulled up in front of the Doresh home and the two stepped out of the car. They walked up the steps of the proch and knocked on the front door.

It was Friday, and Devora was helping Mrs. Doresh prepare the house for *Shabbos.* Rebbe Doresh and Chaim were doing the floor when they heard knocking over the noise of the vacuum cleaner.

"Abba!" Chaim shouted above the noise. "There's some people at the door!"

Rebbe Doresh turned off the vacuum cleaner and went quickly to the door.

"Sergeant! Dr. Sax! So good to see you both. Come on in. Please excuse the mess, we're getting ready for *Shabbos,* as you can see."

The two entered.

"I wanted to thank Devora for solving this whole plot. Not only did she put my mind at ease now, but

she did a great service for the United States government."

Chaim disappeared into the kitchen and came back
with Devora and Mrs. Doresh. Mrs. Doresh greeted the
two men and Devora waved to O'Malley.

"I still can't get used to you in a suit," she said.

"Well," answered O'Malley. "Now that you've
solved Dr. Sax's problems, my assignment is over and
I'll be back in uniform in a couple of hours as soon as I
get the professor settled in a hotel."

"A hotel?" Rebbe Doresh exclaimed. "What's
wrong with our hotel, right here?"

O'Malley turned to Dr. Sax and smiled.

"See, doc? What did I tell you?" He said.

"No, no," Dr. Sax began, "you people have done
so much for me already, I cannot ask you to put me up
for *Shabbos* as well."

"You never asked us," Mrs. Doresh said. "We asked
you."

"Look, professor," O'Malley broke in. "I'll let you
in on a little secret. There's no way you can get away
with a Doresh offer. If they invite you, you can't get
out of it. No scientific formula will help you, either."

Dr. Sax smiled.

"Well, then, okay. In fact, that will give me more
time to thank Devora properly for what she's done, and
to apologize to her for thinking she was silly when she
first told me her theories. I guess, I've been thinking too
highly of my own intelligence. I'm always in charge of

experiments and I'm the one who always knows the answers to everything. Devora, you showed me differently."

"Well, that's what *Shabbos* is for," Rebbe Doresh said. "One day during the week, when we're supposed to step out of our own little worlds and remember that we're part of a much greater world, that of *Hashem*. *Shabbos* reminds us who we are."

"That's just what I need," Dr. Sax sighed.

O'Malley was about to go out and bring in Dr. Sax's suitcase, when he noticed a shiny black limousine parked behind his Ford.

"Hey," O'Malley exclaimed. "Who's this? The President of the United States, or something?"

Mrs. Doresh looked out the window.

"Maybe it's Captain Vernon from the FBI," She suggested. "He called earlier and asked if he could come and see 'Miss Devora,' he said. First, he asked if this was a 'detective agency.' I said no, and he didn't ask anything further."

The doorbell rung and Rebbe Doresh opened the door. Captain Vernon walked in and showed his badge to Rebbe Doresh. He then spotted Sergeant O'Malley and Dr. Sax.

"Hey, what are you two doing here? Seems, wherever I go, you two are always there. I'm here to see Miss Devora, the detective. Who are all these people, O'Malley? Clients, or something?"

O'Malley cleared his throat and looked up at the

ceiling. Devora stepped forward and introduced herself to the stocky officer.

"I'm Devora," she said. The captain was unimpressed.

"Sure, kid. Where's your mother?"

"I'm her mother," Mrs. Doresh said. "And this *is* Devora."

The captain put his hands on his hips and looked at Devora. Then his eyes moved to O'Malley who was still looking for a place to hide.

"O'Malley, I'm giving you five seconds. Where's this detective you told me about?"

Sergeant O'Malley walked over to where Devora was standing. "This is she, sir. Devora Doresh the detective."

Captain Vernon pulled a half-chewn cigar from his pocket and was about to light it when Rebbe Doresh came over and whispered to him.

"We really don't like cigar smoke, captain. Maybe wait until you're outside, if you don't mind."

"Oh, sure, sure. Sorry." The captain said, returning the cigar to his pocket.

"So you're Devora, eh?" he started, looking at Devora. "You're the one with all the solutions, eh? Well, I've got to hand it to you, kid. I mean, 'Detective Devora.' I doubt if we would have figured out what you figured out if we had another year to work on it. You did an excellent job. Really. Who could have imagined an oral "gold bug"?

"Thank you, sir." Said Devora.

The captain appeared disappointed.

"I just feel bad, though, Devora, that because this whole thing is a top-secret thing, there's no reward or anything like that. And I'm sure you were looking forward to a great reward and a free trip around the world or something."

"No I wasn't, captain," Devora said. "Our Talmud teaches us to do *mitzvos* not for the purpose of getting rewarded, but just for the actions themselves."

"*Mitzvos?* What in San Juan are *mitzvos?*"

"Oh. That means the commandments of our Torah, you know, Jewish law."

"Yeah? Jewish law tells you to solve mysteries?"

Devora chuckled.

"Well, not exactly, sir. Jewish law tells us to help other people if we are capable of doing so. And also, we are supposed to do whatever we can to help our country."

"Yeah? Jews have a religious law like that? I thought Jews were just supposed to be loyal to Israel?"

"We are taught to appreciate the host country in which we live, captain, because we're only guests here. The Torah teaches us appreciation on different levels. When we learn to appreciate the host of the country in which we live, then we can better appreciate the host of the universe in which we live, G-d. Everything in life is a lesson, an exercise."

"Yeah? Is that so? You're a pretty smart young lady.

I may want to call on you again if we ever have some dragging cases."

"Hold it, captain," O'Malley broke in. "Devora is already taken. The local police force is using her."

"Well, look at it this way. O'Malley. If we can borrow you from the police force, we certainly can borrow Miss Devora here."

The captain shook Rebbe Doresh's hand and was about to extend his shake to Mrs. Doresh, but she kept her arms to her sides.

"We . . . uh . . . we don't shake hands with men," she said.

"Oh no?"

"Well, with our husbands, yes, but not other men."

"Oh yeah? Interesting. Very interesting. Never heard of that. How do you like that? Interesting."

The captain turned to the door and waved farewell to everyone. O'Malley said good-bye and followed behind him. Dr. Sax was escorted by Rebbe Doresh to the guest room, and everyone resumed their preparations for *Shabbos.*

The Disappearance of
Tom Screvane

evora and her friend, Shaindy Nussbaum, were about to close their *Chumashim*[1] when a police car drove up in front of the Doresh home. Devora and Shaindy had been sitting on the lawn reviewing the *parsha*[2] as they had done almost every Sunday during the summer months when they were not on a trip.

"Oh, no," Shaindy lamented. "It's a police car. I guess that's the end of our plans to play this afternoon."

Sergeant O'Malley stepped out of the car and saw Devora and Shaindy getting up from the grass. He waved at the girls and walked straight for the front door.

"See, Shaindy?" Devora remarked. "He's just going to see my parents, that's all. If he had a case for me, he would have come over to us. He walked straight to the door."

"Why would he want to see your parents?" Shaindy asked, "unless he had a case for you?"

1. Plural term for *Chumash,* the text of the Five Books of Moses.
2. Weekly portion of the Torah read in the synagogue on the Sabbath.

"Beats me." Devora answered. "Let's go and find out."

"I'll race you." Shaindy challenged.

The two girls ran across the grass to the front door of the house. Shaindy reached the door first and stopped on the step of the porch, nearly out of breath. Devora caught up with her and both girls laughed.

"You win, Shaindy," Devora confessed. "I guess I don't run too well when it's hot."

The girls walked calmly into the house and Devora returned her *Chumash* to the shelf in the living room. In the kitchen, Mrs. Doresh was serving a small plate of home-baked strudel which O'Malley was very fond of. Rebbe Doresh sat across the table talking to the officer as they both ate the delicious strudel.

"So you want to take Devora with you?" He asked.

"I really would like to, Rabbi, but I need your permission. It'll just be for a couple of hours, you know, just to check the place out, sniff around for some clues. You know what I mean."

Devora and Shaindy walked into the kitchen.

"Oooh!" Exclaimed Devora excitedly. "Where am I going, Officer O'Malley?"

O'Malley was about to answer her, but he changed his mind.

"Uh . . . I'll let your father tell you" he said.

Rebbe Doresh tapped on the table with his forefinger and then looked up at his wife who was leaning against the washing machine.

"Nu, what do you think?" he asked her. Mrs. Doresh shrugged and bit her lower lip.

"If you want to go along, it's fine with me," she said.

Rebbe Doresh's eyebrows flew up.

"Me, go along? I'm not a detective. But I guess, well, I have a couple of hours to spare. Okay, I'll come along so Devora can go."

O'Malley's face beamed.

"Great. Devora! How do you feel today? Feel up to doing a little detective work with me and my new deputy."

"Your new deputy?" Devora asked. "You mean my father?"

"That's right. As a sergeant, I have the authority to make a deputy out of anyone I wish, for a 24-hour period."

The officer removed his cap from an adjacent chair and handed it to Rebbe Doresh.

"Here, Rabbi, put this on. It's got a badge on it."

Rebbe Doresh put the cap on over his *yarmulke* and everyone started giggling.

"I'll take the case, sergeant," Devora said.

"You will? I didn't even tell you anything about it, yet?"

"With my father as deputy, I really don't care what it's about. Let's go."

"Yes," Rebbe Doresh agreed. "Let's hurry with this case. The hat is getting uncomfortable already."

Rebbe Doresh went to get his jacket and O'Malley showered Mrs. Doresh with praises over her strudel. Rebbe Doresh returned and the three left the house and stepped into the squad car.

As O'Malley drove onto the parkway towards the suburbs, he began briefing Devora on the details of the case.

"This whole thing," he said, "is about a missing kid. A ten-year-old boy. Name's Tom Screvane, Jr. You probably heard of his father, Tom Screvane, the Vietnam War hero who just returned about five years ago. Remember him? He was in the papers for several weeks. He was a prisoner of the Viet Cong for more than a year and no matter how much they tortured him, they could not get a word out of him. All they got out of him was, listen to this: baseball scores! He's a big fan of baseball. So he memorized all the scores from the games of the entire year. But the Viet Cong, ha! they thought he was telling them a secret code, or something. But as soon as they found out what it really was, they hurt him more. But he wouldn't give in. Strong guy, that Screvane. He was a captain. He's still a captain in some ways. A big boss. Owns his own corporation now. Electronics. A millionaire now."

"So now someone's kidnapped his son for money?" Devora tried to guess.

"Nope. I mean, well, we don't know yet, see. We just know the kid's gone. Vanished."

"What's he like," asked Devora, "do you know anything about the boy?"

"Well, from what we've pieced together so far, Tom Junior is an only child. His parents are separated pending a divorce settlement. So, he spends half a year with his father and the other half with his mother."

"What do you know about the mother?"

"All we know is that she's interested in art. She paints. And the boy, he takes after his mother more than his father. He loves to paint."

Devora kept silent and watched the roadside scenery as the car sped along the highway. Rebbe Doresh kept adjusting O'Malley's hat over his *yarmulke,* trying to get it into a comfortable position.

"When did Captain Screvane notice his son missing?" Devora wanted to know as the car pulled off an exit onto a narrow road.

"Yesterday afternoon. He was conducting some kind of business meeting with some special guests from different parts of the world. Tom Junior was supposedly in his room then, but at lunch time, no one could find him. They didn't worry at first. You know kids. But at dinner time, when Junior still wasn't around, they began to worry a little. Then nightfall came, and he was still gone. Boy, did they begin to worry! Even the international dignitaries who were there, began searching the grounds. But no sign of Junior. Come morning, and a whole night's search turned up nothing. Well, Captain Screvane is a tough guy, but he really has a soft heart for his kid. At least I think he does. He called us right away."

"Why did he call *your* precinct? You're not assigned to Long Island."

"Well, he didn't want word getting around too soon. Things like this hit the newspapers so fast, you know. My precinct chief is a personal buddy of his."

Devora looked at her father and couldn't help but smile.

"It doesn't look real on you, Abba," she said, looking at the cap.

"What are you saying?" Rebbé Doresh joked. "Why doesn't it look real on *me?*"

"Your long beard doesn't go with it. It looks funny."

"Devora, my dear, G-d willing, some day you will go to Israel and see men with longer beards than mine, walking around in uniforms."

The car slowed down in front of a high stone wall and cruised along until it reached a huge iron gate. A guard emerged from a narrow booth and approached the car. Walking over to the driver's seat, he peered at Sergeant O'Malley.

"Private property, officer," he said. "What is it you want?"

"O'Malley's the name. We have an appointment with Captain Screvane."

The guard peered into the back of the car at Rebbe Doresh in his cap.

"And who's this guy?" he asked. "And the girl, what about her?"

"The girl's helping me on the case and that's my deputy . . . uh . . . her father."

"Okay. Hold it a moment," the guard said, scratching his head. He walked into the booth again and called the information into the house. After a brief pause, he hung up the telephone and returned to the car.

"Okay. You can go on." He said, waving the car through the gate. O'Malley drove up to the front of the huge mansion and parked near another car, bearing diplomatic license plates. On the side of the car, a small flag extended, blowing in the breeze. It bore a picture of a curved sword.

"Yemen," Rebbe Doresh remarked, stepping out of the police car with Devora. "That car has a Yemenite flag."

"There are Arabs here?" Devora asked.

"Well, like Sergeant O'Malley said, Captain Screvane has guests at his house at this time from all over the world. For business, of course. I'm sure it's got nothing to do with politics."

The three walked up to the big rounded door and O'Malley rang the doorbell. A tall, slim man with a deep tan opened the door.

"Good morning, sir," O'Malley said. "Sergeant O'Malley here. Is Captain Screvane in?"

There was a pause for what seemed to be a long time.

"I'm Captain Screvane," the man said, his face expressionless. "Who are these people with you?"

"Oh, uh . . . well, this is Devora Doresh, and this is my special deputy for the day, Rabbi Doresh, her father. See, the girl's helping out on the case. And because of her age, we have to take along one of her parents."

"She's helping out on the case? You trying to make childplay out of this case, O'Malley?"

"No, no, no, Captain Screvane, not at all. Just give her a chance. She hasn't lost a case yet. I know it all sounds strange to you now. But just wait."

A shorter man of darker complexion approached from behind Captain Screvane. He wore a small black beard and a thick mustache.

"Oh, this is Abu Kharid," Captain Screvane said with a half smile. "I hope you don't mind his being around, since you're obviously Jewish."

Rebbe Doresh smiled warmly and extended his hand.

"*Shalom Aleichem,*[3] Abu Kharid," he said, "welcome to the states." The Arab took Rebbe Doresh's hands reluctantly and then gripped it tightly and smiled.

"Salaoam," he said.

Captain Screvane was taken aback.

"What's going on?" he said, puzzled. "Seems like you two know each other or something."

3. "Peace to you": A traditional Jewish greeting.

"We do," Rebbe Doresh said solemnly, his eyes seeming to stare across a great distance. "We are of the same father. Abraham. You might say we're first cousins."

Captain Screvane shrugged and moved on down the hall, motioning to O'Malley and the Doreshes to follow. He took them to a large, messy room and waited for them to enter. Inside, they found a tall, burly man with heavily greased red hair going through the drawers of a small desk.

"This is Ray," Captain Screvane said. "He's my what-you-call 'security' man. He's trying to find some clues as to where Junior might have been taken. He'll show you around now and I'll meet you later in the study. I have some phone calls to attend to."

Devora felt uneasy about Ray. There was a bulge beneath his jacket which obviously represented a gun. She looked at her father, who was also staring at the bulge in Ray's jacket.

"Well, folks," Ray said after Captain Screvane had disappeared down the hall. "This is Junior's room. We found it just the way it looks now. It's not like Junior to leave his room a mess like this. We think he probably has been kidnapped."

Devora walked slowly around the room, trying to get an idea of what kind of boy Junior was. She walked over to the boy's closet.

"It doesn't look like any of his clothes were

removed," she said. "What's behind this other door here?"

"Oh, that?" answered Ray, breaking into a grin. "That's Junior's art-supply cabinet. How do you like that, eh? A ten-year old boy who paints pretty pictures all day. He doesn't play ball, doesn't like to wrestle; all he wants to do is paint, paint, paint. A real sissy, that kid."

Devora's nose wrinkled. She did not like Ray's attitude and she began to sense that perhaps this was Captain Screvane's attitude as well. She inspected the shelves of the art-supply cabinet and accidentally knocked a pack of cards onto the floor. Each card had a picture of a famous baseball star and a record of his game scores.

"I gave them to him," Ray said. "I told him it would make his dad real proud if he would memorize the scores of each player. Know what I mean? His dad's a real baseball nut."

Devora swung around facing Ray.

"Can you show me some of the boy's paintings? You never know. They might contain some clues."

"How's that?" Ray asked, a little annoyed at being quizzed by a young school girl. "The kid was kidnapped. The only clues would be fingerprints, not what he was painting."

"Why do you think he was kidnapped?" Devora asked.

"What do you mean? What else could have happened?"

Devora walked over to the open window of the room, which overlooked a wide patch of lawn leading to the main road.

"Maybe he ran away," she said.

Ray looked at Rebbe Doresh and smiled.

"You know, mister, you got a bright kid, here. But she's way off track. One of the detectives who came down this morning before you did, said the same thing. Captain Screvane kicked him out of the place in a hurry. The captain's given the boy everything he could ever have wanted. There's no reason why he would have run away."

"The question is," Rebbe Doresh began, scratching his beard, "whether the father was giving the son everything the *son* could ever have wanted, or everything the *father* wanted. That's the question. A boy who likes to paint will surely find some conflict living with his father for six months when his father thinks that painting is a sissy thing to do. Maybe Devora is right."

Ray did not say anything more. He simply sighed and pointed to the boy's bed. A small pile of canvasses lay on the bed. Devora went over to the bed and started examining the paintings. As she lifted the canvasses individually, she noticed they had been ripped down the middle. Ray came up behind her and crossed his arms.

"See, Miss?" he said, "they're ripped. The kid

would never have done that to his own paintings, now, would he? There's no doubt he was kidnapped."

"Was a ransom note found?" O'Malley asked.

"Neh. These things take a couple of days. You know that. Kidnappers usually wait a few days, maybe a week, before coming up with the ransom request. That way, they figure the parents are really desperate by then and scared enough to give them any amount of money they ask for."

Devora looked at the paintings carefully.

"These paintings," she remarked, "they seem to be the work of two different people. Some look pleasant and others look like they were made by an angry artist."

Ray chuckled to himself.

"That's just what the other detective said this morning. He was a psychologist cop, see, and he said that Junior was torn between doing what he liked to do, painting, and pleasing his father by being rough and manly. But soon's he said Junior ran away, the captain told him to leave."

Devora sat on the bed, looking through the remainder of the paintings. As she rose from the bed, she heard a thud. Something heavy had slipped to the floor from behind the headboard.

Ray unfolded his arms and knelt by the bed to see what had fallen. Sergeant O'Malley and Devora crouched beside him. Ray pulled a large sheet of canvas from beneath the bed, contained inside a heavy wooden

frame. O'Malley helped him maneuver the large painting from between the feet of the bed and stand it up
against the wall. It was a picture of a baseball player
holding a bat, ready to hit a ball.

"Wow," Ray said, impressed. "Looks like Junior
copied this one from the cards I gave him."

Devora walked over to the supply cabinet and came
back with the cards. She flipped through the pack until
she found the one which resembled the man in the
painting. She held the card in front of Ray's face. Ray
looked at the card, then at the painting and then back at
the card. Devora watched his face. He seemed
impressed now by the artistic talent of Tom Junior.

"Come with me," he finally said, lifting the painting and walking out of the room. The trio followed
Ray through a carpeted hall to a brightly lit oak-
paneled room with a large heavy desk in the center.
Captain Screvane sat behind the desk, his back to the
group, a pearl white telephone held to his ear.

The captain swung around on his leather swivel
chair and faced the group. But gradually, his eyes
trained themselves on the painting of the baseball
player.

"Uh . . . Richard," he said into the telephone, his
eyes fixed on the huge painting in front of him. "I'll . . .
uh . . . I'll call you back later, right? No, no, no.
Nothing's wrong. I'll . . . uh . . . I'll speak to you later,
okay?"

He placed the phone on the shiny black receiver and spoke while staring at the painting.

"That painting," he said, "where did you find it?"

"Behind the headboard of the boy's bed, sir," Ray said.

"Junior did that one, too?"

"Yes, sir. It seems like he did."

Tom Screvane got up from behind his desk and stepped in front of the painting. He looked at the tense expression on the player's face.

"Looks like . . ." he started to mutter, "looks like, you know what it looks like? By golly, he looks like he's about to hit a ball high in the sky and dash right out of the frame across the field. This is good! Real good! This isn't sissy stuff, Ray, look at it. My boy's got real talent."

Devora took a few steps toward Captain Screvane.

"Captain Screvane, I don't believe your son was kidnapped. I believe he probably ran away. But for a little while. He'll be back soon."

Captain Screvane's proud expression turned into an angry one as he listened to Devora's remarks.

"No." He said. "It can't be. Tom and I love one another. We're very close. He has everything! A big room. A ten-speed bike. A wide area to run around in outside. A gym downstairs. A swimming pool, everything! Why does everybody think he ran away?"

O'Malley cleared his throat.

"Uh . . . sir, let me explain. See, Devora feels that the boy certainly loves you very much, just like you say. He therefore found himself caught in between what *he* wants, that is, to paint, and what *you* want, which is to play baseball and to involve himself with sports and other rough, challenging activities."

"And so away he ran, eh?" Captain Screvane asked in a gruff voice. "Hogwash. Makes no sense. I mean, if that's the case, why would he ever want to come back? And also, why would he make this painting of a baseball player?"

O'Malley looked at Devora and then back at the captain.

"Captain," Devora said, "because Tom Junior wanted to try very hard and please you, he thought that maybe he could use his artistic talents to do just that. So he tried to paint the baseball player you see here. But he was probably afraid to show it to you. Maybe you wouldn't like it and then he would be too disappointed to try some more paintings. He wanted very much to make sure that the first sports painting he was going to show you, was going to be the best. This way, he probably hoped to resolve *your* interests with his own."

Captain Screvane took a deep breath and sighed.

"What you're saying makes nice sense, kid," he said. "But it doesn't answer questions like, where is he now?"

"I would bet," said Devora, "that he went to a special art exhibition in town that they're having this week. It happens to be an exhibition of sports in art. There, he is hoping to learn new and better ways to make the first sports painting he shows you the very best one."

"You're talking out of your nose," Captain Screvane said. "How do you know? You're some kind of prophet, or something? How do you know there's an exhibition going on?"

Devora smiled and opened her clenched right fist. Everyone looked eagerly into her hand at a small piece of notebook paper, folded several times.

"When we looked underneath the bed to pull out this painting here, I spotted this little note lying near his slippers. He must have dropped it, or maybe it fell out of his pocket. It has all the details, the name of the exhibition, the dates and location."

Captain Screvane took the note from Devora and unfolded it gently.

"You're a clever detective, Devora. But I don't understand why he would stay away overnight. That's what disturbs me most."

"He probably feels he can't return till he proves himself," Rebbe Doresh remarked. "He's only ten. He ran away determined to prove himself to you. No sense in coming back before he could do so. That's how a child's mind works. Our Talmud tells of a young man who felt threatened by his father who was overly strict with him. The boy ran away. He felt his father didn't care about him."

"I care about my boy," Captain Screvane retorted.

"You have to make him *feel* that, sir," Rebbe Doresh continued, speaking in gentle tones. "Children are very sensitive. We adults are sensitive. So you can imagine how much more sensitive are children. Jewish law is very strict about that, you know. A Jew is not allowed to break anything on the Sabbath, for example. But if a young child is locked in a room, frightened, even though there is no danger to his life, the door must be broken."

Some commotion was suddenly heard in the front lobby of the mansion. Captain Screvane brushed past O'Malley and Rebbe Doresh and walked quickly down the hall toward the front.

"Tom!" He shouted half way down the hall.

Everyone followed behind the captain as he rushed toward a tired, but happy Tom Junior. Father and son embraced tearfully.

"I'm sorry, dad," the boy cried. "Really I am. I won't run away again."

"It's okay, Junior. Forget it," the captain said.

Abu Kharid came in and joined the happy group. Standing in the doorway was an elderly man with a big stomach, a short white beard, wearing a brown beret.

"Dad," Junior exclaimed. "This is Charlie, from the exhibition. There's an exhibition in town, full of sports paintings. He spent an entire night with me in the studio that they have near the exhibition. He was showing me all kinds of ways of painting sports activities.

And you know what? He's the one who makes the pictures on the cards."

"Been at it for thirty years," the man said, smiling. He then stepped away from the door and extended his hand to the captain. Captain Screvane shook his hands.

"The boy's got great talent, Cap'n. Better encourage him. Look at these." The man withdrew a rolled-up bundle of canvasses and unrolled them one after another in front of the captain. The captain's eyes opened wider with each painting.

"Got a phone book?" The old man asked. "A thick one."

Abu Kharid went over to the telephone desk and took a Manhattan Yellow Pages from it. He gave it to the artist. The artist put the paintings on a chair nearby and held firmly onto the phone book. Then his face turned red and his arm muscles began to bulge and everyone watched in amazement as the phone book was ripped in half.

"Captain," he said. "Being an artist does not mean you can't be 'manly'. And being 'manly' does not mean you shouldn't paint. We have an old saying, 'Who is the mighty one? One who is able to conquer his moods', take control of himself, do what's right no matter what. That's what's most important. King Solomon once said that that is a more important quality of strength than being able to conquer an entire city."

"I've been hearing wise Jewish sayings all morning," the captain remarked. "What are *you* telling me?"

The artist smiled.

"Some more Jewish wise sayings. Charlie *Goldstein's* the name. And let me tell you, you got a tough kid here. He was determined to let nothing stand in his way until he was able to get the best painting accomplished. I kept interrogating him, asking him where he lived, his phone number and so on. But he wouldn't budge. Said nothing. Just wanted to learn to paint better."

Captain Screvane hugged Junior again and then looked admiringly at Devora. Rebbe Doresh shook Charlie's hands and answered his questions about what a rabbi was doing in the mansion and wearing a police cap yet.

"I wish to thank you folks for everything," said Captain Screvane, walking over to Rebbe Doresh. Rebbe Doresh shook his hand. "Especially you, Devora," he continued. "More than just solving a mystery, you have all helped me to see my relationship with my son in an entirely new light."

"Same here," Abu Kharid interrupted. "You have made me see my relationship with my *cousins* in a whole new light. I never did think too favorably about Jews, you know, with all the anti-Israel propaganda with which I grew up. But you have been refreshing models for me of what Jews are like."

"If only you could now convince your fellow countrymen," said Rebbe Doresh, "that we're not the aggressors they think we are. We all have our differences, you know, Jew and Arab, even father and son.

But most of those differences are based on major mis-understandings of one another. If we seek to find the good in things, we will succeed, if we don't, it could be staring us straight in the face and we wouldn't know it. Tom Junior never ran away. He only sought to do away with misunderstanding. Now he will be able to continue painting, and still please his father."

Glossary

Baal Shem Tov — Rabbi Israel Shem Tov (1700–1761), founder of the Hasidic movement.

b'ezras Hashem — with G-d's help.

Birkas HaMazon — grace after meals, recited after meals when bread is eaten.

Boray nefoshos — Who created many souls. A blessing recited after partaking of most types of food or drink.

bracha — blessing over food, said in gratitude to G-d.

challah — a specially baked loaf of rich bread, eaten with the Sabbath and Festival meals and used as part of *kiddush*.

Chumash — Five Books of Moses, the first five books of the Bible, or any one of them.

Chumashim — the plural form for *Chumash,* the Five Books of Moses.

daven — pray.

halacha — Jewish law.

Hashem — G-d, lit. the Name. This term is used to avoid using the proper name of G-d.

kabala — the secret teachings of the Torah.

kaddish — a prayer that G-d's Name be magnified and sanctified in the world. It is recited by mourners during the first eleven months after the passing of a parent and on the anniversary of their passing.

kiddush — blessing recited over wine on Sabbaths and holidays before the meal.

maariv — evening prayer.

matzah — specially baked unleavened bread, eaten during Passover, in commemoration of the Exodus from Egypt and the unleavened bread that the Jews ate then when they were in too great a hurry to bake normal, leavened bread.

megillahs — scrolls.

mezuzah — lit. doorpost. A parchment scroll enclosed in an encasement, affixed to the right doorpost of any entrance. On this scroll are written the sections of the Bible, prescribing this rite, namely Deut. 6:4-9, 11:13-21.

Midrash — a number of books, containing homiletic interpretations of the Bible.

mincha — afternoon prayer.

minyan — a quorum of ten adult males, required for the recitation of certain prayers, such as *kaddish*.

mitzvah — an act required by Jewish law or committed within the spirit of Jewish law.

parsha — weekly portion of the Torah, read in the synagogue on the Sabbath.

Passover — a holiday falling on the fifteenth day of *Nissan* (around mid-April), commemorating the Exodus from Egypt 3,000 years ago. In Israel, it is observed for seven days, whereas in the Diaspora, it is observed for eight days.

Rambam — an acronym for Rabbi Moses ben Maimon, an outstanding twelfth century Talmudist, philosopher, and physician.

Rashi — an acronym for Rabbi Shlomo Yitzchaki (Rabbi Solomon the son of Isaac, 1040-1105). Author of the most popular commentary on Bible and Talmud.

Rosh Chodesh — beginning of the month, the first day of the Hebrew month, proclaimed on the New Moon.

Rosh Hashanah — New Year according to the Jewish calendar. It falls at the beginning of the month of Tishrei, which usually coincides with late September.

Shabbos — Sabbath, day of rest. The seventh day of the week, designated for rest, to commemorate G-d's resting on that day after creating the world.

Shalom aleichem — "Peace to you." A traditional Jewish greeting.

Sh'ma — an important section of the Torah read every morning and evening (Deut. 6:4-9, 11:13-21 and Num. 15:37-41).

shul — synagogue.

siddur — prayerbook.

Sukkos — Festival of Booths, a holiday commemorating G-d's protection of the Jewish people during their 40-year journey through the desert on their way to the Land of Israel. *Sukkos* falls on the fifteenth day of the month of *Tishrei*. As part of its celebration, all adult males and children who can get along without their mother, are obligated to live in a temporary dwelling, a *sukkah,* which must have a minimum of three walls and a temporary roof made up of detached grass or branches. This covering should be thin enough to allow one to see the stars through it. This is to remind the celebrant that G-d is his ultimate roof and protector. The holiday of *Sukkos* is observed for seven days in Israel, after which *Simchas Torah* is observed. Outside of Israel, the *sukkah* is used on the eighth day, although the eighth day is known as *Sh'mini Atzeres,* and the ninth day *Simchas Torah.*

tefillin — phylacteries, a pair of leather boxes, containing parchment scrolls upon which certain sections of the Bible are written, viz. Exodus 13:1-16, Deut. 6:49, 11:13-21. These boxes are bound around the arm and the head, and worn during the morning service.

tzadik — a very righteous Torah Jew.

yarmulke — a skullcap, worn by Orthodox Jews at all times.

yahrzeit — anniversary of one's death. For observance of parents' *yahrzeit,* see *kaddish.*

Yom Kippur — Day of Atonement. This falls on the tenth of Tishrei, eight days after *Rosh Hashanah.* Jews fast on this day and pray during the entire day for forgiveness of wrongdoings committed during the past year.

Yom Tov — lit. "good day." It is a term used for the periods of a holiday during which no work may be performed, like on a Sabbath. Thus, the first and last days of Passover, for example, are called *Yom Tov. Rosh Hashana* and *Yom Kippur* are also called *Yom Tov.*

Acknowledgements

I am grateful to many people without whose editorial assistance this second volume of the *Devora Doresh Mysteries* would still be on the planning board.

—Gershon Winkler for his many imaginative and insightful contributions.

—Rabbi A.J. Rosenberg for his constructive criticism and editing.

The practical editorial contribution of Ms. Bonnie Goldman as well as the efforts of Ms. Devorah Kramer, who responded artistically with talented illustrations, deserve my warm and sincere thanks.

Particularly, I wish to express my gratitude to Mr. Jack Goldman of Judaica Press whose faith, encouragement and invaluable guidance spurred the swift continuation of this series.

C.K.H.

Temple Israel

Minneapolis, Minnesota

IN HONOR OF THE BIRTH OF
JONATHAN KENNEDY
FROM
RABBI STEPHEN H. PINSKY